I WILL
FOLLOW

I WILL
FOLLOW

EIREANN CORRIGAN

Scholastic Inc.

Copyright © 2024 by Eireann Corrigan

All rights reserved. Published by Scholastic Inc., *Publishers since 1920*. SCHOLASTIC and associated logos are trademarks and/or registered trademarks of Scholastic Inc.

The publisher does not have any control over and does not assume any responsibility for author or third-party websites or their content.

No part of this publication may be reproduced, stored in a retrieval system, or transmitted in any form or by any means, electronic, mechanical, photocopying, recording, or otherwise, without written permission of the publisher. For information regarding permission, write to Scholastic Inc., Attention: Permissions Department, 557 Broadway, New York, NY 10012.

This book is a work of fiction. Names, characters, places, and incidents are either the product of the author's imagination or are used fictitiously, and any resemblance to actual persons, living or dead, business establishments, events, or locales is entirely coincidental.

ISBN 978-1-339-00288-0

10 9 8 7 6 5 4 3 2 1   24 25 26 27 28

Printed in the U.S.A.   40

First printing 2024

Book design by Christopher Stengel

For my sisters, the first girls I followed:
Maureen McKay, Kathleen Ryden, and
Christine Corrigan

CHAPTER 1
NORA

The first time Shea Davison surfaced on my screen, she danced a ballet, hip-hop hybrid that had my feet moving below my seat. She cleared leaps that I'd only seen other creators make with trampolines and ice skates. She performed like a professional but she talked like me.

Lots of dancers have their own channels. And so do lots of teenagers. But Shea is both. She creates all the typical content— but what I love most about watching her is the joy she takes in all of it. Sometimes she dances alone and sometimes she features her friends. Shea is okay with sharing the spotlight and her fan base respects that a great deal.

Clearly, she's not auditioning friends based on talent. Half the time, they're muddling through the routines. But Shea just smiles even wider. To be honest, I feel strongly that her friends drag her down. If you're going to ride coattails, you'd better at least keep up. I could dance alongside Shea Davison and as long as I really put my heart into it, I'd fit right in.

Just her presence would encourage me. You get the sense that Shea and her friends walk around town and suddenly start dancing. Like *West Side Story* but without all the gang violence.

As her top follower, I glean whatever details I can; I've trained myself as an excellent detective. Shea drinks a lot of boba. She prefers to wear green. She talks incessantly about her mom and her friends; she never discusses boyfriends. Shea refers to her mom as brave and that says all it needs to about her father. She never mentions her dad. He barely comes up at all.

No one watches Shea Davison as closely as I do. No one notices like me. But when the videos end, my window narrows and shuts. I can't help her from this distance. We need to meet in person. We need to get to know each other. To trust and inspire each other. We need to become best friends—entwined and inseparable.

That will happen with me and Shea.

I'm her best friend. She just doesn't know it yet.

I am so close now. I have practiced and practiced—imagined each step and executed accordingly.

Everything is falling into place now. Everything is going according to plan.

CHAPTER 2

SHEA

We are so close now. It's been ages, it feels like. Imagining the steps, executing the routine. Now, with all the bodies in motion, with the music bouncing off the studio walls, everything is falling into place. Everything is going according to plan.

"I gotta say, none of this is working for me," Delancey shouts over the music, stepping out of formation and stalking toward the speaker. The music cuts out abruptly and a sudden silence hangs over the bare room. Heads swivel my way, waiting for me to react.

"Maybe we need to work through the steps a few times," I say. "We have to keep at it."

"We *are* working at it," Delancey shoots back. "That's my point. If it feels like work, it looks like work. Dance should flow."

"Eventually, yeah. But we have to learn it before it flows." I catch myself and try to drain my voice of any trace of expertise.

Delancey won't tolerate that. "Listen—" I try to make eye contact with the whole group. "It's not going to click right away for anyone."

Diana rushes to reassure me. "I see you clicking, Shea. Don't sweat it." I don't even need to glance over to know Delancey's rolling their eyes. Beneath the music, beneath the beat of any song we choreograph, this is the real rhythm running through our dance team—the pull of Diana and the others agreeing with every one of my ideas, and the push of Delancey rejecting those same suggestions. I can count on each like a metronome, but neither is very helpful.

For the longest time, I danced on my own. I hit record just to check my positions. Then I started experimenting, trying to break through my ballerina box. That's when I began posting online. That's when it all changed.

I have a ton of followers. Out loud, I always maintain it's no big deal, but maybe that's not completely accurate. Those followers get us free weekly hours at the studio. Free gear from the Movefree label of dance-inspired athletic wear. Sponsorship and product placement money that goes straight to my college fund.

Some of the people in this room, who I'd swear are the best friends I've ever had, arrived once my numbers started climbing. Those friends followed my followers.

Except Delancey. Delancey and I have always compelled each other. They have watched me dance since I scampered across a stage in my first recital. Their mom made them present me with my first bouquet.

And now their dad is about to marry my mom. It's the kind of plot twist we might have dreamed up during sleepovers and playdates. Now, in high school, it's complicated. Delancey keeps unleashing capital-F Feelings. I'm trying to keep up.

Gently, I try to pinpoint today's problem. "Maybe," I say to Delancey, "if you could describe what's not working . . ."

"None of it."

Great, I want to say. *That's an easy fix.* But instead I count the beats off to myself, the way I might count off waiting for a piece of music to start. Here comes Delancey singing the soon-to-be-stepsiblings blues.

"If you want to know the truth—" They pause. The rest of us look miserably at each other because here comes the truth, whether we want it or not. "I don't understand what this dance has to do with my dad's wedding."

Diana gasps theatrically. Pearl presses her lips together. Jolie stares at the ground.

"You mean our parents' wedding," I say.

Delancey shrugs. "I mean they're going to have a first dance, right? It's a wedding. Lots of people are going to dance. Lots of people will be eating cake. Are we going to choreograph a routine for us eating cake too?"

"I thought we both wanted to do this. Our parents want us to do this. They both seemed excited."

5

Diana says, "Of course they seemed excited. Who wouldn't be excited? It's a beautiful gesture."

I wish we could talk alone. I wish Delancey would tell me what's really wrong. The others look expectantly at us, waiting for the two of us to work it out.

"Do you not like the music?" I ask.

Delancey sighs. "It's fine. Let's just start from the beginning."

We run through the routine a few more times. We line up and cross each other precisely. We bump hips and grapevine out to our separate corners and then run a cascading line of snap rolls. I try to rally. But my feet feel heavy now. The lightness I'd felt pirouetting across the floor drags with questions.

Delancey's drama tends to do that lately—deflate me. Ever since our parents announced the engagement, they veer from manic excitement to barely suppressed rage. I'm just trying to keep up.

It's different for me. Delancey's dad isn't replacing anyone. At least anyone worth anything to me. After everything Mom and I dealt with after my dad left, I would have been thrilled with anyone who made her happy.

About a year ago, Mom sat me down to tell me that she'd made a commitment to see some guy exclusively. She insisted he come to dinner, implied that I needed to approve. And then the dude turned out to be Delancey's goofy dad, who swore a lot in traffic and packed them weird junk food lunches. Mom was confused by Delancey's deadname, by all the changes over the past few years. Maybe that stung too. Maybe Delancey felt unrecognized. Or unnoticed. But I thought we'd moved through that, sorted it all out.

But maybe Delancey feels differently.

The song sails through its crescendo. We hold our final positions until the music ends. "We're getting there," I proclaim, bending with my hands on my knees, relishing a good stretch.

"We're already on the honeymoon!" Diana calls out, all amped up.

"How did that feel, Delancey?" I ask.

"That felt great." Their words are still flat. "I'm just glad that it's a live performance—a memory that Dad and your mom can keep for themselves."

Let it go, I tell myself.

But Jolie cocks her head to the side and says, "What does that mean?"

"Just that," Delancey replies. "It's their wedding. It's not a public event. So we shouldn't record it."

At first I don't understand what Delancey's saying. Then I do. It's like that moment when you're out on the water. The weather called for rain earlier. And then you see the dark clouds gather above you.

"We have to record it," I say. "To post it."

"Shea, it's a family moment. It's not your content."

"We've talked all along about recording it."

"*You've* talked about recording it."

We volley back and forth, and I understand, by the way they fire back responses, that Delancey has already argued this with me several times. Alone in their room. In the shower, beneath the stream of hot water. It's just that I am finally here for it. And I am floundering.

Of course, Diana comes running to save me. "We've all talked about recording it. From the very beginning." She has a lot at stake here. Most of my videos are just me—the branding executive advised the importance of keeping the channel's focus on me. A group dance that I promised to post on my channel on a Thursday night—a high-traffic time slot—is amazing exposure for everyone involved.

"It's important that some things stay private," Delancey states.

But why this thing? I want to ask. *And why are you deciding this during our fourth rehearsal?*

"We've talked to our parents," I remind Delancey and reassure the others. "They were all about this plan. Our dance is a gift for their wedding. And we talked about posting. We even decided on Thursday night."

"You mean you and your mom decided."

My mind races to remember. We were all sitting around the table. Mom had her laptop out and we mapped out the night's event. Even a small wedding is a large-scale production. "Delancey, you were right there."

They sit back then and fold their arms in a way that says I've confirmed their argument. Their bizarre and unexpected argument. It's not like Delancey is a completely private citizen. They're my best friend. They show up all the time—in my life and on my channel. More than anyone in the studio, they should understand that this is part of the unspoken contract.

Viewers devote time to you. They feel attached. Most of my followers discovered me while my mom was dealing with a really difficult time. Now my mom has found love again. Completely randomly on Tinder. With my best friend's dad. Had Delancey and I scripted that plot twist, no one would have believed it. But because viewers watched it all unfold in real time, right along with us, they're invested.

"Listen, we need to post the video. I'm sorry that suddenly bothers you, but everyone here signed up for that. We've talked about this as a family. I know my mom's on board and I'm pretty sure your dad is too. There's a wedding countdown. People have even bought gifts off their registry."

Delancey throws their arms up in the air. "Yeah. They have . . . and that's *bonkers*."

The other dancers are shuffling around the studio, making it seem like they're trying not to listen but obviously taking in every word. I crouch down next to my soon-to-be-stepsibling and speak quietly. "I don't know where this is coming from, but can we please talk it out on our own?"

They consider it. Our faces loom close enough to each other

that I can see the vein pulse near their right eyelid. I know them well enough to understand that they're mulling my words.

Finally, they say, "Don't worry about it, Shea. We'll do it your way. We always do." My mouth opens to object, but Delancey's already queuing up the track. They sigh. "We better keep practicing." The other dancers snap into position. "If we're going to go viral, we'd better at least be good."

We're halfway through the ninth run-through when the studio door swings open. Diana stumbles first, and then Jolie. Pearl does not even look up. Delancey moves to stop the song.

At first, I figure it's the owner of the studio. Maybe she wants a selfie. Then I wipe the sweat from my eyes, and see the girl who's interrupted is young like us. She's wearing dance gear— last season's Movefree line. I recognize the half shirt as one I plugged on my channel.

"Can I help you?" I ask.

She looks around. "Sorry. So sorry, but I rented this space? Studio Two?"

"But you didn't," Diana blurts obnoxiously, and the girl looks like she's about to scale the walls.

"I mean, I did. For six thirty."

"Nope." Diana sidles over, her hands on her hips. "The studio rents by the hour. At least that's what I've heard from the people who have to pay. Our time here is comped. And we're comped until we feel finished."

Delancey catches my eye. *Rein in your monster, Dr. Frankenstein.*

I step forward, partially to put space between Diana and the other girl. "I'm so sorry," I say. "There must be a mix-up. We're definitely here until seven; I set it up with Madison at the front desk."

The girl shifts from one foot to the other. "Yeah, Madison sent me in. She said there was a dance class but that you'd wrap up soon."

"Dance class?" Diana sputters. "Take a look around."

Delancey steps forward. "Diana means we're a professional troupe. We've reserved the space until seven, but you're welcome to stay and watch." Their eyes flicker to me when they add, "We're not, like, married to the concept of privacy or anything."

Delancey knows how much I hate rehearsing in front of other people. Even rehearsing with a dance team feels challenging sometimes. In ballet, I'd spend hours at the barre, perfecting my movements before rehearsal even started. I can't stand everyone watching me while I figure out a routine.

I don't want this total stranger to watch me stagger around the studio.

"We can call it a night," I say, heading to the hooks on the wall to grab a towel.

Jolie and Pearl fall out of form. Diana mutters about interruptions and needless drama. Pearl chugs from her water bottle, then says, "Today didn't feel very productive. I've got college applications due in two months. Could you and Delancey please figure out the family dynamics before our next meetup?"

"Of course. Pearl—I'm sorry." But she's already out the door. Diana takes her sweet time to pack up. Jolie and Delancey are working through some steps in the corner. The other girl still stands on the opposite side of the room. She has a small duffel bag. I don't see a speaker but maybe she'll just play music on her phone.

She sees me looking at her and says, "I don't mean to rush you. It's just that I'm losing time."

"Yeah. I get it. We're packing up."

The girl watches my friends as they slowly float around the room. The whole thing is awkward. "What kind of dance do you do?" I ask her.

That perks her up. "Mostly street. Hip-hop." I don't understand how she doesn't recognize me. I'm not obnoxious; it's a matter of algorithm. If this girl's on TikTok at all, she has definitely seen my videos.

"Cool, cool," I say. "Please don't let us stop you. If you want to get started . . ." I gesture at the open floor, but the girl doesn't answer or make any effort to move. We both just stand there watching Jolie and Delancey go through the routine.

I buckle first. I call out, "You guys, I think we really need to head home."

"So lame." Diana glares at the hip-hop girl.

"Thanks, Di. We really got through so much. Next rehearsal, we'll nail down that last configuration."

"I'll FaceTime you when I get home and we'll talk through

it. I got you, girl." She moves to scoot by us and brushes past the newcomer. "Sorry, not sorry!" Diana sings as she heads out.

I want to sink into the smooth wooden floor. "Listen, I want to apologize—"

"No need."

"It was just a weirdly emotional rehearsal for a lot of reasons—"

"I just really need the space."

Okay then. I'm caught between this girl's righteous anger and an upcoming excruciatingly tense car ride home with Delancey. I call out, "Hey, you two, we really have to head out."

"Oh—I figured you were talking." Delancey jogs over. "Jolie and I were just working out that last sequence. I mean, we want it to be perfect, right?" They turn toward the stranger standing beside me. "Shea's mom and my dad are getting married. We're creating a dance for them as a gift. Well, Shea is, but we're there to support her."

"Oh wow. That's cool. Congratulations." The girl speaks in a flawless monotone. She could not possibly sound more bored about this news.

"I mean, all of us are giving them the dance," I correct for Delancey's benefit.

"But really it's Shea's thing. Maybe you know Shea?"

Hip-Hop Girl can't even bring herself to look at me. She doesn't even pick up on what Delancey means.

"Sorry, I don't," she says. "I'm pretty new in town. We just met. See you around." With that, she goes to the barre and begins to stretch. She does not turn around, but I swear, she watches us in the mirror, waiting for us to go already.

"Okay," I say, "we're done here." Jolie's long gone and I steer Delancey out. "I don't know why you had to do that?"

"Do what?"

Delancey knows exactly what, but I say it anyway. "You raised concerns and I listened to you. You didn't need to illustrate your point. There was no reason to tell that weird girl about our dance. Or about Mom and Bryan's wedding."

"Gosh. If only we had printed cards to hand out, with our parents' wedding registry. At least then maybe we'd get a free blender out of it. I'm sure that weird girl who clearly didn't care at all about the cultural phenomenon that is your channel will spend all night deep-diving into Google for traces of you." Delancey snorts derisively. "No, you're right—I am so sorry to have shared those private family plans with a random stranger. But maybe you'll luck out and she'll look you up online. That's just what you need, right? 920,001 followers."

I used to think a number like that would make me feel awesome and powerful. But when Delancey spits out stats this time, they don't mean it as praise.

It sounds like an accusation.

CHAPTER 3

NORA

Adults don't advertise enough how awesome and powerful it feels to carry a ring of keys around.

I don't need to ask anyone's permission to take a walk in this cute little neighborhood. No one critiques the way I'm dressed. The ring of keys weighs my pocket down in a particularly pleasing way. Once in a while, they jangle faintly.

Sometimes I catch a glimpse of myself in a store window and feel amazed at what I see. I look just like any other girl shopping and strolling. In Olympic Coffee, I order a flat white in a bored voice so that the barista thinks I stop at cafés all the time. The foam machine chuffs and surges and I try not to hear my father's voice growling beneath it. *Wasteful*, he'd say. *Like you're too good for Folgers.*

The girl who takes my order asks my name and I say Indigo just to see her scrawl it on the cup—a drink for a more glamorous version of me. "I love that," she says. "Do people call you Indy?"

"My friends do, yeah."

Indigo glides down Sixth Avenue. At the vintage consignment shop, she holds up an orange chiffon blouse and doesn't assume it will look ridiculous on her. She smiles distantly at everyone. She browses the used paperbacks at the hospital charity store, and when the old man who works there asks if she's a student, she nods and says, "I just started at University of Puget Sound."

I am so caught up in being Indigo that when my phone rings and I see it's my older sister, Helen, I answer as if it's the best idea in the world and not a decision fraught with danger. "Helen!" I practically shout into the phone. "How ARE you?"

"All good here, Nora. You doing okay?"

"I am. Just out and about—really enjoying the gorgeous weather." I'm talking to my older sister but I'm performing for the people walking alongside me, the other reflections shimmering in store windows.

"Okay . . . great. I'm happy to hear that. Where are you out? Are you in town? On your own?"

And then suddenly the phone call gets so much easier. Because I realize that my father hasn't told my sister I've left town. Sonny might not even realize I'm gone. I mean, he's most likely missing his truck. But if he was worried, he would have called Helen right away. A delay indicates a slow burn of rage that will undoubtedly flare up eventually.

For now, though, I just need to catch up with my big sister.

"Well, you know I'm in Spokane." Of course she doesn't know that. Of course I am not in Spokane.

"Wait, what?"

"I'm sure I told you. My gaming friend. We planned a meetup. I'm just visiting for the long weekend. It's so great to meet her in person."

"Sonny let you sleep over at someone's house?" The complication of this story is that Helen also grew up on the ranch. More than anyone, she understands how unbelievable this possibility is.

I sell it with the casual cool of a girl named Indigo. "Well, it's Kylie, my gaming friend. We know each other so well. We talk every night."

"But you've never met? Hold on a sec, Nora. Macon? Macon, honey, please don't drive your truck through that. The dog drinks out of that." I hear Helen shuffle around the receiver. Her voice wheezes with effort. "So this Kylie—you met in person for the first time when you showed up in Spokane?"

"I didn't just *show up*. She invited me."

"Right. I get that. And this online stuff, I guess people do that kind of thing all the time these days. I just can't believe Sonny went for it. He let you go there. Good for you."

Helen sounds so genuinely happy that it kills my mood. Because eventually she's going to remember this conversation and know I lied to her.

"Macon, honey, please don't put cereal there. Sorry, Nora. It's

17

great that you're meeting Kylie. But how are other things going? You're still keeping up with your health promises, right?"

"Yeah, I am."

"Yeah? Good. Like how?"

"Helen, can we talk about this another time? I'm at my friend's house."

"Yeah, sure. But there's always going to be stuff going on, right? And that's why we make health promises. We make space for taking care of ourselves. We've talked about that. You know I scheduled a Zoom call with Dr. Forero. Can you just confirm it's on your calendar?"

"It's definitely on my calendar."

"What day?"

Walking along Sixth Avenue in Tacoma, a girl named Indigo floats over the concrete. Nothing touches her. Strangers smile at her. The voice on the phone sounds distantly insistent.

"Nora? What day?"

"Helen, I have it written down. You emailed me the link. It's just that I'm at Kylie's house right now and I can't talk to you and look at the calendar at the same time."

Helen sighs. "I get it; I do. This is important, though, Nora."

"Right."

"Because you know it's important to build that relationship with your therapist, to hold yourself accountable."

"Right."

"Here's the thing, Nora: I know how hard it is to live with

Sonny and still remind yourself on a daily basis that you are strong and capable and deserving of love. In other families—well, let's just say that message comes across more clearly. But Sonny is just one part of your life. Your life is your own. You get to take care of yourself by eating healthy, getting good rest, and accessing your other nurturing resources. Therapy, medication, even me—we are all nurturing resources. Macon, honey, could you please just let Mommy talk to her sister on the phone?"

Objectively, ask anyone and they will tell you my sister, Helen, is a good person. She strives to be patient with her children. She pays for my therapy and finds a way to arrange for it that doesn't threaten Sonny's ego or worldview. She genuinely worries about my welfare all the way from her house in Southern California.

So I aim to be patient with Helen and give her the reassurance she needs. "Thanks for setting everything up. I promise I won't miss my session. The appointment makes it so much easier." I rattle off my talking points and remember yesterday's studio session, how it felt to finally stand in the same room as someone so important to me. Instead of just watching a screen, I could see her in person. Explaining how amazing that was to my sister feels impossible.

I still try. "Helen, I hardly ever have a chance to leave the ranch. And now I'm out here with a friend. I get to see where she lives. I'm meeting her other friends—"

"I know, I know. That's really great, Nora. It kills me to put any kind of damper on it. I just want to make sure you're okay—that's all."

"Of course I'm okay. This is the best weekend of my life."

"I bet." My sister speaks quietly, in the voice she uses to tuck her little boy into bed. "Enjoy every minute. Remember to thank Kylie's parents and make good choices."

"Of course, Helen. I love you." I look down at my feet positioned at the crosswalk, feel the reassurance of a ring of keys in my pocket.

My sister has never met Indigo.

"Aw, Nora. I love you so much. Okay, I'll let you go now. Take care."

I drop the phone in my bag and picture my sister falling into the darkness, her dumb face frozen in permanent worry. Back home, calls from Helen are my lifeline. They're a strand to the outside world I can always grasp. Sonny never forbids those calls. It's important to keep up family ties, after all.

Usually, Helen spends the entire time describing Macon and Ben's latest escapades and whatever latest project she's got going at her house. She tells me about paddleboarding in ocean inlets or how she's redoing the backyard again in hopes of achieving the perfect outdoor kitchen. She'll pepper me with questions. Am I eating all right? Is Sonny serving me warm food or MREs? But mostly she's reminding me that there's a life waiting for me after Sonny's bunker. I just have to grow up a bit more to get there.

In Tacoma, a girl named Indigo has decided she's waited long enough.

CHAPTER 4

SHEA

If anyone has any doubt whether my mom counts as one of the kindest people alive, they only need to look at the front porch of our house. She decorates it for every holiday with a themed tablecloth and little ceramic animals. And that's great and all. It's adorable. But my mom also keeps a wicker hamper on our porch. She fills it with ice-cold water, protein bars, and fresh fruit. She leaves bottles of sunscreen in the basket and even masks and sunglasses during wildfire season. There's a whiteboard there where she writes a different thank-you message each week.

To be fair, we get a lot of deliveries. Lately, there's an occasional wedding present. For the most part, though, the packages are coming for me.

Inside the house, I find my mom in the kitchen, sorting through the day's deliveries. She's designated the side counter as the donation area and puts the few keepers on the kitchen table. Beneath the table is the laundry basket where she places those items that she thinks I should feature in my videos—the clothes or sneakers, accessories or beauty products. Today there's a giant beanbag spilling out of the laundry basket. It's beige velvet with bulging plastic eyes.

"What's that?" I ask.

"It's a pug," my mom replies, like that explains everything.

"Okay, but it's giant."

"It's a beanbag chair. Don't you think it's adorable?"

The pug chair looks like it's being asphyxiated. It's got a crazed look. "Yes?" I ask her.

"I thought it was very sweet. And it must have cost a fortune just to ship." I stand there and wait. I know my mom will eventually arrive at an explanation. "I know you probably won't feature it in a video."

"Mom, most of my videos are dance videos. Right?" She doesn't respond. "That's a chair."

"Maybe you could sit in it and talk about dance a little bit?" She sighs then and throws up her hands in resignation.

Not for the first time, I wonder what people are thinking when they send me some of the items they do. For one thing, it's not easy to find my address. We're not fully locked down or anything but it's not like it's prominently displayed on my channel. People or companies have to make an effort just to track down the mailing address.

I do feature *some* items; at least one video a week sees me wearing an item received from my viewership. That's more than most channels do. Mom and I have met influencers who totally outsource their mail. We respond to almost everyone. Unless there's some creep factor involved, Mom insists that I write a thank-you note to everyone who sends me a gift in the mail.

As I write my latest round of thank-yous, I realize this is a good moment to bring up what Delancey said yesterday.

"Hey," I say, "was the idea of us all doing a dance at your wedding off base?"

Mom looks surprised by the question, which is a good sign. She says, "I love the idea of a dance at the wedding. The whole point of a wedding is the dancing."

"But maybe the point is for you and Bryan to dance? Maybe it's not the best time for a Shea Davison number. You know?"

"I *don't* know. Where is this coming from?" Mom asks. I don't say anything. I picture Delancey staring me down, folding their arms in the corner of the studio. "Shea, the wedding isn't just about Bryan and me. Weddings are about families. I think it's lovely that you'll be sharing your talents. Had you'd kept up with flute lessons, I would have expected a flute solo. But my daughter happens to be one of the best-known dancers on the planet. I'm honored that you'll dance at the wedding."

"But maybe we don't need to broadcast it. If you and Bryan want your privacy, we don't have to post a video."

"Don't be ridiculous. People love weddings."

Mom stands up and starts fussing with the packages in the donation pile. "You've got an extremely loyal viewership, Shea. But that's not accidental. I think you're finally starting to realize what a great dancer you are, and I'm glad for that. But do you know what you are even better at?" My mom slaps the kitchen counter. "Marketing. Brand building. You are ahead of your time. Lots of people can dance in front of a carefully balanced phone. You've reached people. You've opened up your life and built relationships. Your viewers relate to you. That's not an accident. And it's not easy. Don't let anyone minimize that."

She doesn't say Delancey. But my mom looks at me and holds eye contact and I know we're both thinking: Delancey.

"Thanks, Mom." I sigh.

"Of course." She nods magnanimously. "Besides, I got a discount on the flowers because I mentioned they'd appear in the background of the video." We cackle then, standing in a kitchen packed with freebies. Maybe we are kind people. But maybe we are also pretty much living down to Delancey's vision of us.

Mom says gently, "We're all going to have some adjustments to make. We knew this. Bryan and I were so focused on the fact that you and Delancey were such good friends, maybe we haven't taken enough care with this transition. But it's completely reasonable for you both to have fears and misgivings about the ways our families are about to change. Try not to take it personally. I won't. Neither will Bryan."

"Thanks, Mom."

"Yeah, yeah. Don't thank me. Thank the person who sent you the pug chair." She nods at the stack of cards beside me. "As a matter of fact, thank that person right now."

When I'm done, I nurse my cramped writing hand in my own room. I've got a lab to finish and a full chapter of Global Politics to read. Nothing holds my attention beside my phone, though. I keep waiting for a text from Delancey, but they've gone quiet, even on the dance team group chat.

I don't sign in to TikTok. When I start yawning, I force myself up into the wide space of my bedroom to dance—not really because I need the practice but because I need to wake up.

I'm practicing spins when I notice the calendar. The one on my wall is just like my mom's wedding planning system downstairs. But instead of her bridezilla to-do list, mine plans my channel's future: contest dates, product placements, new routine debuts. The writing for this coming Friday doesn't match the rest of my careful printing.

I know they probably wrote it weeks ago. Maybe tonight they're not quite in the mood to joke, but it still makes me laugh. They must have snuck it onto the board when I wasn't looking. The entry for Friday reads *normal adolescent fun*.

I'm still laughing even as I hit call. "I need assistance with something on my calendar."

"Yeah?" Delancey replies grudgingly. We have some ground to cover still. "It's okay if you have plans."

"This Friday? So sorry. I have some kind of family thing going on."

"Gosh, that sucks for your family." I can hear the smile in their voice.

"What counts as 'normal adolescent fun'?"

"You don't even know anymore, do you?" There's no right way to answer so I wait for Delancey to tell me.

I don't have to wait long. Their excitement spills past this afternoon's resentment. It overcomes tonight's distance. "Friday night," they announce triumphantly, "we are going to the state fair."

CHAPTER 5

NORA

I smell the fair before I see it. That says a lot about the way the aroma of kettle corn clings to the air. The Ferris wheel reaches deep into the sky and still I notice the sweet smell of caramelized sugar and maple before I see anything resembling a carnival ride.

Tacoma may feel unfamiliar to me, but I am right at home at the state fair. Of course, it's bigger than the one thrown by Whitman County, but that's just acreage. Fairs all feature the same components, after all—versions of the same rides, games hawked by the same grizzled barkers, the same food fried in vats of sizzling oil.

I arrive early enough that it's mostly moms and their preschoolers toddling through the entrance gates. I tuck Sonny's truck away in a corner, in the shadow of a row of tall pines. The woman at the ticket booth asks to check my bag. My mouth dries up and my throat closes, but she just blindly riffles through its contents. I'm a tiny girl wearing sunglasses and a Seahawks cap. I'm no threat to anyone.

Right now, the greatest danger to my plan is my dwindling cash reserve. I remind myself to be careful with expenses. It's easy to eat your way through a fair. Each booth tempts with a different treat; but you're paying for the experience, the once-a-year delicacy. My belly grumbles hopefully every time I pass another stall. I don't need to eat yet. I fill up by taking it all in.

More people are present in the approximately five square miles of the Washington State Fair than I may have seen in the past five years living at Sonny's ranch. The air feels thick with the presence of these strangers, the breath they exhale, the space they take up. My nervous system hums, primed to react. My skin tingles. My eyes ache from keeping my lids open. I don't want to miss anything.

I slip my sunglasses into my backpack. No one will recognize me here. I walk the entire perimeter and try to note each exit. As the day passes, I try to keep track of the ways the pedestrian traffic follows a pattern. The lines stretch longest at the booths closest to the front entrance. Most of the women pushing baby strollers exit through the crosswalk closest to the school parking lot. Groups of people congregate near the restrooms by the food halls. The porta potties on the edge of the petting zoo seem relatively empty, but the handwashing station is a sudsy mess.

The corner of the fairgrounds where I feel most comfortable

should be the livestock display and rodeo. But it's hard to tour those tents without thinking of Sonny.

"You seem like you're fixing to measure those sheep. You looking to purchase?" The voice ambles over from an old-timer leaning against the side of an RV parked to the left of the pig and hog tent. I go still. I don't want conversation. I don't want to be noticed.

"No, sir. They just remind me of home." We used to keep a lot of animals. Back in another life, when the ranch seemed like a place for my parents to build a life together. Helen even raised alpacas for 4H. I'd help her haul out the buckets of feed. I remember how their eyes would follow us, from the minute we stepped out the back door until we'd stuff the windrows with fresh hay.

"Well, you seem to have a good eye for a healthy animal. Your family have some land?"

"A little bit." That's what Sonny would say, chatting with folks at the Agway in town. He'd never name how much or talk about the land up in Packwood. *A little bit*, just like the way he'd answer the waitress at the Sunset when she asked if he'd like gravy on his mashed potatoes.

The old man tips his hat to me. It's a large felt cattleman, worn at the brim. Sonny hangs his hats on a row of hooks on his bedroom door. "I like to see a young person appreciate the animals," he tells me. "Not just stand there with her phone out, taking those selfies with the camera."

"Oh no, that's not my thing." I laugh as if that's the most absurd thing ever. Farm girl like me. We stand there in companionable silence and watch the fair swirl around us.

"No school today? You seem like a bright girl. I don't figure you for skipping school."

"I'm here with my classmates actually. We're taking measurements of the roller coasters for physics class."

"Are you really now? They sure do school differently nowadays."

I smile my friendliest smile. At Sonny's ranch, I did school all year round. The desk pushed into the corner, stacks of books, a list of approved websites, and carefully monitored homeschool chats. The only classes I took in person were jiu jitsu and archery.

But the kind old man doesn't need to know all that. He's just making conversation. He doesn't really care that I've only watched science labs on YouTube. I haven't tackled a group project since the fourth grade, when my mom still packed me lunches and waited with me at the bus stop.

I feel a little dumb now, standing on the edges of the fair, sequestered with the herd animals. This isn't why I've taken so many risks. I didn't steal Sonny's truck and blow my savings just to stand next to an old cowboy and talk ranch.

I push off the fence. "You have a great day, sir."

"Already done," he drawls. "You enjoy the fair."

Already done. I make my way past the tent where you can

hold a baby piglet, then the pen in which the little kids wander around with wire brushes combing the goats. Every time I pass another animal, I travel farther away from my father.

The sun closes in on setting. I remind myself: My plan is thoughtful and careful. I arrived early to take stock of the premises, to walk the perimeter and map out routes through the crowds and the chaos. Now I know. I move confidently.

I even put down a five-dollar bill to throw three darts at a wall of balloons. "Ladies and gents—she's an ace shot." I don't duck from the attention. I just smile and shake my head slightly. Refuse the prize and step back to disappear into the crowd.

It's getting dark. The moms are pulling their wagons toward the exits. The fairgrounds are filling with teenagers and maybe even college kids. People closer to my age—either version of me. I make sure to cover a good distance from the rodeo before I take my cell phone out and snap a few selfies. I don't want to shatter the old cowboy's wholesome image of me but the glow of the Gravitron looks otherworldly.

Near the amphitheater, folks have already begun to line up for the night's first performance. But I don't need to get so close. Not quite yet. For now, I'll just hang back and support from a distance.

Behind me, some punk kid with mismatched Vans and a board beneath his arm mutters to his friend, "Why are people lining up for seats already? People need to keep MOVING." He bellows the last part obnoxiously, as if expecting the crowd to part in front of him. Sometimes I wonder how other people take up so much space in the world. How they just blare their voices into the world, figuring that other people want to hear them.

His friend says, "It's just some influencer. Nobody really."

I clench my bag to my side and keep my eyes fixed forward. No one has lined up at the state fair to see Skaterboy and his friend careen down the metal railing of a public staircase. None of their ollies or kickbacks or whatevers have gone viral. *It doesn't really matter*, I remind myself. *Not everyone will understand.*

CHAPTER 6

SHEA

"Mom, this doesn't matter even a little bit." We hunch over in the back of the RV and my mother fusses over my hair.

"It matters to the folks waiting to see you."

"Maybe exactly four people. And hopefully their night doesn't hinge on my hair."

"I guarantee you—more than four people are lining up to see you. And had you and Delancey given me any lead time at all on this, we would have been able to advertise. I'm not saying a billboard, but we could have at least gotten in a few ads." Mom holds a braided strand of my hair in one hand, the brush in the other. She's got a tortoiseshell barrette pinched in her lips. When she gets animated, she gestures, and her right hand pulls my hair from my scalp.

"You're hurting me."

"Sorry." I feel her patting down the sore spot on my head

so that it doesn't look red and inflamed in pictures. "But, Shea, really, had I known you wanted this, we could have applied for the mainstage."

"We didn't want this." Delancey clips their words short. "We wanted to go to the fair like normal fifteen-year-olds."

"I promise it's a quick performance—not even a full song—followed by a short meet and greet. You give your fans the chance to see you and then they'll give you some space and let you have the night to yourself. Think of it as a compromise."

Mom's grip on my hair loosens a little. "Okay, listen: I'm sorry I just went ahead and made the booking. But I did and it's a legal contract. And you shared it on TikTok, right? So that's a different kind of contract. You made a promise to your fans." Mom finishes fastening the barrette, then sprays my hair. "It's a quick half hour—forty minutes, tops. Next time, I'll talk it through with you."

"I get it." I'm not even mad. It just means dealing with Delancey being mad. "Thank you for setting it up, Mom." Delancey shoots me a look more bitter than the hair spray hanging in the air.

"Could we possibly be ready now?" they say.

My mom replies, "You look great too, you know."

"Yeah, yeah, we all look like stars." They say it sarcastically but at least they smile the tiniest bit. The thing is, we probably *do* look like stars, climbing down the steps of the RV. The parking lots are full with Friday night crowds, but when Mom pulled out her phone and showed them the QR code from the fair organizer, we were waved right through by the traffic attendants.

The thing is, I happen to feel talent lot–worthy tonight. My hair looks cute. I'm wearing a set sent by the Fabletics rep that isn't even available on the website yet. It's mint green with a jade stripe running down each side. And then my sneakers have soles in that same shade of jade. I don't see people really doing green. When Mom and I attended the marketing consult, the woman kept talking about signature colors and that seemed really cheesy. But I see the allure now.

Mom reaches her hand out to shake the hand of a staff member who peers out at us from a booth by the stage. "I'm Kallie—this is my daughter, Shea Davison, the dancer."

"Hi, Shea!" the woman in the booth says brightly. "We're so glad you could make it."

"Happy to be here!" I smile widely and make eye contact.

"You've got quite a crowd already," the woman says. (Mom can't help herself. She looks back and raises her eyebrows at Delancey.) "We couldn't give away tickets to the Doobie Brothers. We had to bus in folks from the retirement centers over in Kirkland. Older folks just don't want to gather so much—even for an outdoor show. I don't know how you got the word out, but you've got young people lining up for over an hour now."

My mom glows. "Well, you know Shea has over nine hundred thousand followers, so when she posts . . . it's like a tidal wave of teens." *Oh god.* I cringe. I don't even dare look toward

Delancey. My mom just said *tidal wave of teens*. "We learned in the past year that it's better to start the music first, then have Shea start performing. Can you show me the sound system? Shea, Delancey—I'm going to ask you both to hang back while we get everything set up. We don't want to excite the crowd too early."

"Of course," Delancey says drily. "Anything to avoid a riot." We step into the booth. It's wooden, with a built-in counter and a bulletin board in the back. I see a Post-it Note tacked to the board with my mom's cell phone number scrawled on it. Delancey gestures to the space beneath the counter. "Do you think you should hide from the rabid crowds?"

"I'm sorry—she just gets so excited." I feel a pang of hurt. I've worked hard for this. I'm not about to admit it to Delancey, but I'd like a chance to get excited about it too.

They're my best friend. Maybe that's how they read my mind. Delancey sighs and reaches out to squeeze my arm. "I'm sorry, but there's no way for me to get away from this now. Before it wasn't so much. It wasn't constant or so in-your-face. And even then, I could go back home and take a break if I needed to." And now their dad is marrying Mom. Delancey doesn't need to draw me a diagram.

"Listen, Del, we said it was amazing how this all worked out. The chances of it—and, come on, my mom loves you." Delancey levels a look at me. I backtrack but only slightly. "You know how much she cares about you. I get that it feels complicated. But she's not trying to replace your mom. She's just excited to be your stepmom."

"Yeah, I agreed to a stepmom. I didn't sign up for a momager."

I open my mouth to argue. But then Mom climbs up on a picnic table in a distant corner of the fairgrounds. She waves frantically at us and then more theatrically toward the crowd. Faintly, the first few beats of my intro music crackle through the loudspeaker. I hear my mom bellow, "Are you all ready for Shea Davison?"

"Showtime," Delancey murmurs, and I launch into my slow jog toward the small stage inside. Like any live performance, it feels ridiculous for the first minute or so, but then I see people, mostly girls, clapping and nodding and moving along with me and I let myself go. I'm careful to make eye contact, to say, *Here I am, make sure to watch me carefully.* I let the music take over and carry me away from my self-consciousness. I let go of Delancey's dramatics, the pressure of my mom watching me from the far corner of the amphitheater. I just dance.

The wood planks of the stage floor vibrate with the music. I feel it in my feet. The crowd moves with me. It's like an electrical charge buzzing beneath all of us. The faces around me blur. When I need to ground myself, I look down at the green soles of my sneakers. We're always careful to choose a song that's been shared a lot, but then vary the moves.

When I'm done, I let my eyes focus for the roar of cheers and applause. My mom smiles widely, her hands in the air. The crowd has grown. I throw my own arms up and bow and then work the front of the crowd, giving half hugs or just touching outstretched hands.

Mom taps her headset to switch on her microphone. "Thank you, Washington State Fair. I know Shea is so glad to join you tonight." She pauses; I nod vigorously. "If you're here for Shea tonight, we know you already follow us. But if you just showed up for the sick beats, then you might want to check out her channel for more fresh content." I roll my eyes and smile to let everyone know I'm cooler than my mom. Mom keeps hamming it up. "We've got some time before those candy apples start calling our names. Until then, Shea's going to hang around to meet y'all. Please feel free to introduce yourselves. Of course we brought along some giveaways too." That elicits more cheers.

It took me some time to master the art of working a crowd. You have to get used to people touching you. You have to make eye contact but not prolonged eye contact. You give compliments but not too many and they should be as genuine as possible. "Love your earrings!" I tell a girl who has enormous turquoise feathers dangling from her ears. "They must be so lightweight; I bet you can dance with them."

She touches a hand to an earring and nods like she's confirming they're real. "I hardly feel them." I nod and smile and move on to someone else.

You can't actually spend time getting to know anyone. Most of the people who come out to my appearances are kids younger than me anyway. If it's a grown man by himself, I nod politely and move on to engage with a girl closer to my age. I'll sign papers and shoes but no body parts. You can't really radiate seriousness when you say no, though. Instead you act like it's hilarious because of course they must be joking.

You have to take selfies. It doesn't matter if you feel bloated or you're dealing with a breakout. Selfies are necessary. If someone's really awesome, I'll record a dance with them. Not a whole song, but a few bars, a few moves. Something they can boomerang.

Mom and I always plan out a reason to leave. Tonight will be a little tricky. We'll need to disappear and let the crowd thin out before we can walk around the fair in peace. Knowing my mother, she has that all set up. She walks by me, nods approvingly at the way I'm working through the throng, and silently hands me a bottle of water.

When the crowd around me finally dwindles, Delancey steps forward. I don't have to turn around to see; I just sense them closer. That's how connected we are.

They hold up their phone and tap its screen. "Our real friends have arrived. It's time for some normal adolescent fun. You promised—"

"I know, I know," I start to say, but then see that the last part was aimed at my mom.

She nods, a little tightly, but she still nods. "Of course! You all go have fun. I want to circle back to Miss Chelsea over at the entertainment booth and see if we can't schedule something for the mainstage next year."

"Mom—"

But she holds up a hand, palm out, warding off my arguments. "It can't hurt to ask. And if next year feels different, well then, it feels different."

That's the closest Mom gets to acknowledging that all of this—the free stuff, the appearances, the followers—it's all pretty temporary. People move on quickly, especially my demographic. We can build my brand all we want, but we're building on quicksand.

Delancey grabs my shoulders to steer me away. "Sounds good. Let's go. Jolie and Diana said to meet them at the Ferris wheel."

We tumble away together then and leave my mom to her ambitions.

"Oh my goodness," Delancey says. "Thank you, fleeting gods of celebrity. Are you sure we can mingle with the general public? You don't need me to hold a velvet rope around you as we walk?"

"Stop." I hate when Delancey talks like this. My face goes hot with shame and embarrassment. In my head, I translate my best friend's sarcasm: *Who do you think you are?* "I'm sorry that took so long." Silence. "Some of it's a little bit fun, though, right?"

"Nope. None of it's fun."

"Dance is fun," I offer.

Delancey sighs and wraps her arm around me. We lean forward as we walk. I wear my hood up, hoping no one recognizes me and also hoping Delancey doesn't realize I am making that effort. Their arm squeezes my shoulder. "When was the last time dancing honestly felt fun for you, Shea?"

"At the studio. During rehearsal." I don't say, *Except for the part when you yelled at me.*

"Rehearsal was *not* fun. Your mom has commodified a part of life you love. The minute you went from being a girl to being a brand, dance stopped being fun."

"Not for me," I say, firm in my reply.

Delancey says, "If something is so fun, why not just do it for its own sake? Did we not learn anything from our adventures in ballet?"

I feel a strand of anger start to thread its way through my rib cage then. Delancey knows more than almost anyone in the world about how dance first spun sideways for me. We took our first ballet classes together. I loved every aspect of it. The pink leotard, the tights, the soft shoes. I loved the precision of each movement and the smooth wood of the barre beneath my hand. Everything had its right place in ballet.

I was so good at it. Our teacher brought in another teacher to see me. They called in my parents for a conference. They added classes to my schedule, hours of practices to each week. After two years, they recommended a new school to my parents—in Seattle. It was imperative that I work with the best teachers early on in my training. It could change the trajectory of my career in dance, they said. I was eight.

Mom went all in. She scaled back her hours at work to drive me to practice. She monitored my diet because the instructors had praised my body's perfect form. Delancey quit ballet when I switched schools.

The Seattle school was entirely different. The Sailish Academy for Classical Dance was internationally ranked in the most elite circle of the ballet community. The teachers reminded us of that fact frequently. Most students didn't even attend school in the usual way. They had tutors; their parents "homeschooled." We danced for hours every day.

I moved quickly from Madame Cloussard's class to Madame Flint's class. Madame Cloussard was strict, but kind. Madame Flint was strict. She believed in cultivating muscle memory. We repeated the same movements hundreds of times in front of the studio mirrors with Madame pacing behind us with a bamboo cane in her hand, slapping her palm on tempo.

The trouble began in my hips and radiated to my knees and my ankles. Madame Flint would advise my mom that my youth was interfering with my talent. I needed to toughen up or return to "hobby dancing." Mom had glimpsed my future as a prima ballerina. It took a while to let go.

By the time she allowed me to quit, the orthopedic surgeon believed my knees were ruined. I couldn't take gym in school, much less go back to my former cheerful dance academy. The Sailish Academy had taught me to be ruthless with my own body, but meek with everyone else. Only Delancey knew how angry I'd been.

So it hurts to hear them toss ballet in the mix, as if it's just another point in our debate. Behind us, I hear the twang of the bluegrass band that replaced me on the stage. Other fairgoers walk by carrying enormous loaves of curly fries in front of them like offerings to the gods of the fair. Kids scream from the Angry Viking ride. I keep my own voice low and measured. "Listen, I really love what I'm doing with the channel. Maybe you can see that better than anyone? It gives me a chance to dance on my own terms again."

"Totally your own terms."

"Del, I need you to be on my side for this." To my complete horror, my voice cracks saying it. A wellspring of tears glimmers under my words.

Delancey squeezes my shoulders again and sidesteps the tearful moment. "Yeah, yeah. I'm sorry to be so relentless about it. We're here to have fun. I insist on so much fun. Okay?"

I take a deep breath.

"Okay. Onward to so much fun. To the Ferris wheel."

Delancey snuggles their face in my neck. "I am always on your side."

We meet up with Diana, Pearl, and Jolie and decide to go on some rides.

We all stick against the wall of the Gravitron and then we ride the Vertigo swings. From that height, everything looks so tiny. I stare down at my own feet, dangling over the fair. My green kicks look like they could stomp on everything.

43

Back on the ground, Jolie and her boyfriend, Marcus, drape themselves over a bench, sharing a funnel cake as big as my face. The rest of us head to the fun house next. It's one of the few attractions at the fair with hardly any line. At first, when we enter, I think it's just us. We make our way up the moving staircase. We slide across the floor and its optical illusion tiles. There's an *Alice in Wonderland* theme going on and I almost pitch forward in the tearoom.

Then we make our way through the hall of mirrors. I see Pearl in the distance, but I've pretty much lost everyone else. I can hear them just fine—Delancey has Diana giggling about something but everywhere I turn, I see only my own reflection.

This would be an amazing place to record a video, even though the mirrors would make filming a pain. I spin a little and take a few quick steps and see that the trouble would be so worth it. The mirrors make every step look amazing. It's disorienting to see so many of me along with the soundtrack of the calliope music playing through the speakers. I set up my phone on the floor, check to see if anyone's around me.

"Shea, where are you?" Diana calls out, a few mirrored corners ahead.

"Hold up, I'm right behind you—I just want to check out these optics."

"God. Stop already. You've already performed tonight, Shea." Delancey's voice sounds more distant and warped with frustration.

"Five minutes. I promise."

Ahead of me, I think I see me again. Or maybe a different version of me. This girl is taller than me but dressed like me. Her green pants don't have the same racing stripes but they're similar enough that I look down to check my own clothes. She moves but the mirrors confuse me. I can't tell if she moves closer until she's right there in front of me. I shake my head.

Across from me, I see her hair flip. She does the same quick steps and kick sequence I just performed in front of the mirror. Objectively, her movements are not quite as tight as mine. That's the kind of observation Delancey would roll their eyes at, but I can't help noticing. The girl steps off the beat just the slightest bit. She looks familiar and not just because she resembles me. I've seen her somewhere before. My mind works in overdrive, but I can't quite place her.

Her dance brings her closer to me. Even when she stretches out her arm, I look to see if it's my own arm outstretched. But it's the girl, the other version of me, reaching through her own reflection. That's when I see something flash in her hand.

Then I feel a needle-stab of sharp pain, a flush of warmth.

The calliope starts to slow and the mirrored wonderland begins spinning.

CHAPTER 7

NORA

I brace myself under Shea's weight. There's no time to appreciate how much we look alike, standing there, arms wrapped around each other, surrounded by mirrors. I have minutes—maybe even seconds—to navigate through this maze and the maze of what comes after.

Half limping, we reach the bag I stashed near the fun-house exit. I wrap my Carhartt jacket around her, lower her hood, and tug a navy ribbed wool cap over her hair. She looks different enough. We might just skate on by. I can't do much about her trademark sneakers or the mint green in general.

We careen through the exit. I don't let myself look toward Shea's friends, who are all gathered by a bench. I've been careful, drifting along the edges of the fair—never too close to the group, but near enough to track her movements. With my hair down, with makeup all done up, they won't recognize me from our run-in at the studio.

"Dude—" I say loudly enough for the workers at the Tilt-A-Whirl to hear me. "You know how sick you get on spinning rides. Know when to stop already. Just try not to puke, okay?"

No one's paying attention, though. My performance is unnecessary. It's amazing to think of the crowd of folks who gathered to watch Shea dance not even two hours ago. And yet no one notices her now.

We move slowly. I wish I could have arranged to meet Shea closer to the spot where Sonny's truck is parked and waiting. The truth is I hadn't meant for all of this to happen so soon. But when Shea posted yesterday after rehearsal that she'd booked a surprise appearance at the state fair, the change in plans felt preordained. Sometimes stars line up just right.

Pretending the studio had double-booked us was supposed to be the first phase of many. That way, Shea would know from the start that I, too, am a dancer. I would keep seeing her around town. That would have made it easier to collaborate. It's going to be more of a challenge, I think, to establish the strong connection we need in these circumstances.

If I'm being perfectly honest, her personality is a little bit disappointing. Shea is self-obsessed in a way I hadn't anticipated. Maybe that's on me—self-obsession probably checks out for a professional influencer. For example, Shea had every opportunity to get to know me at the studio. She didn't ask me about myself at all. She barely registered my existence. None of them did.

Now I get her to the lot before her friends even notice she's gone. I know there are cameras everywhere, so I make it look like we're having a good time together.

It's hard, though, because she can barely walk. She'd just fall to the ground if she weren't leaning on me. Luckily, the truck's in the trees, hidden from cameras.

"It's okay, Shea. You just overdid it," I soothe her. "Don't worry about anything. I'm right here and I'm going to take you home."

"Del?"

"Yeah, it's me. Just let me get you in the car."

It takes all my strength to boost Shea into the passenger seat. Then I buckle her in. "There we go," I say. I reach down into my bag, grab one of the bungee cords, and wrap it around both her wrists tight. She yelps and I tie the knot quickly, binding Shea's hands together on her lap. It's a move I spent a lot of time practicing, and I'm pleased that all my practice paid off. There's no way she'll be able to undo the knots in her current state.

When I slam the door shut, she sits straight up and lets loose this ungodly scream. I look around, but luckily, no one seems to notice—not with the riders yelling from the roller coaster, the screamers twisting on the Zipper.

"Now stop that already," I say when I get in the car. "You're really going to hurt yourself."

"Sthorrrrwy," she slurs.

48

I glance back at the fair gates, half expecting Shea's friends to come sprinting toward us. For the first time, I notice a car with PIERCE COUNTY SHERIFF emblazoned across its doors. It's way past time to get on the road.

I turn the key in the ignition.

"Please, please." Strings of drool hang from the corners of her mouth and snot runs from her nose.

"Don't distract me when I'm driving." Firm and friendly. I carefully back the truck out of the spot and head out. I'm relieved when Shea passes back out against the headrest.

We inch along in the exiting traffic. I stop myself from checking my rearview mirror every ten seconds, from glancing back at the sheriff's car or even the Ferris wheel turning against the night. Shea doesn't look too good. The lot is full of people. All anyone has to do is turn toward the truck and really study her.

Once we fully exit, I finally exhale. Drive a few blocks and then pull the truck over to the curb. I feel Shea wake and tense next to me. Her wrists pull at the cord, but I really did a bang-up job on that knot. It just gets tighter when she tugs.

"Don't do that," I tell her. "It'll just tighten and then you'll need to worry about cutting circulation off to your hands. We don't want that, right?"

I grab my phone and lean my head closer to Shea's. Hold it up to snap a selfie—our first one together. "You know what?" I tell her. "I just need to adjust a little bit." I cover Shea's bound hands with my duffel. Then I hold the phone back up and snap several more pics. "That's so much better," I tell her.

But she's tired. She squeezes her eyes shut and turns to her window.

"I know," I say. "I hear you. Let's get on the road."

CHAPTER 8

SHEA

My mouth tries screaming again but nobody can hear me. No one knows. I'm traveling away from them. On a road I've ridden hundreds of times. Farmers markets, holiday light shows. Every year at the fair. I crane my head toward the window and see the bright lights twinkling behind us.

She sees me looking. "That fair was amazing. I've been to lots, but never to one that big. I bet you always get to go, though." Panic clenches my chest. My throat constricts. Behind us, the fair lights start to fade. I can barely see the top of the Ferris wheel over the buildings. That's our Lost and Found. Mom designated that spot in case we were ever separated in the crowd. *Wherever you are, you can see the Ferris wheel. You just go there and wait. That's where I'll find you.*

I try to read street signs, but my eyelids feel so heavy. I have no control of my body. My mouth tastes so much like cotton, I think at first she's shoved something in my mouth, but it's just my own tongue lolling around, helpless.

She's not much older than me. Her eyes stay on the road. We sit high up, in a truck maybe. I don't remember getting in here. She's going fast, switching lanes with confidence. She says, "The tranquilizer will wear off eventually. I tried it on myself first, to make sure it was safe. I would never endanger you, Shea."

I can't weigh which is more frightening: the word *tranquilizer* or the fact that she knows my name. My wrist throbs. The skin directly under the cord feels numb. My fingertips tingle. *Please*, I try to pronounce. But it just comes out as a moan.

She glances over at me. "Listen, I get it. There's a lot to process. But obviously, I need to drive carefully, for both our sakes. I'm a good driver, but I'm a new driver. I'd appreciate it if you could be considerate. We're going to have so much time to talk, Shea. I promise. Try not to fight the medicine. Just close your eyes and rest."

We're driving along the Puyallup River. I see it, a dark ribbon curling along the road. We head through the reservation and past the Ill Eagle fireworks store. Every now and then I see a car pulled over to the side of the road, an RV stretched in an almost empty lot. No one sees us.

"When you feel more up for talking, you can call me Nora. It's a little odd, frankly, that you wouldn't ask. But I've noticed that about you—I hope my honesty is welcome here—you just don't seem that interested in other people, Shea. It's you, you, you."

My lower lip starts to tremble. I bite it for betraying me. Next to me, Nora does not appear to notice. "There's an us now, though. So let me tell you a little about your new other half. I turn seventeen in December. I dance as well. No formal training. Sonny—that's my father—he would never allow for that kind of 'indulgence.' But that just means I had to work harder to learn.

"Same thing, honestly, with tech. I have so much to learn from you in terms of the platform. And maybe filming. I've noticed that lately you've evolved that aspect of the channel pretty quickly. Lots of new lighting tricks, fresh angles. Really, Shea—your work is *seen*.

"I don't mean to imply that I have nothing to contribute. My goodness, that's not the case at all. I have so many ideas. This cabin has been in our family for years—it's a totally unexpected setting for a new turn in your channel. A collaboration—with me!"

I stare out the window into the darkness and imagine Delancey and the rest of my friends spilling out of the fun-house exit. They laugh and compare selfies and then someone starts to wonder what's taking me so long.

I remember feeling so tired, how my feet felt encased in stone. My armpits burn from where the girl held me up and dragged me. The fun-house doors were marked EXIT ONLY. My friends might have tried the door anyway until someone stepped in and directed them to the front entrance. I imagine Delancey holding up their wristband, impatiently running it under the scan, probably angry at me for holding everyone up.

53

Or maybe Delancey was too angry for all that trouble. Maybe they just rolled their eyes and headed on to wait in the next line. Jolie's favorite ride is the Cliff Hanger. We promised we'd go back when the line was shorter. Maybe my friends decided I would meet them there after I got all the mirror footage I wanted.

I'm thinking all these things, and meanwhile, the girl keeps talking.

"Listen, I'm pretty sure I'm one of your first followers. I'm talking early days, when you were still copying trends and Tik-Tok phrases. So I fully recognize that this kind of partnership is a departure. But honestly, I think it's exactly what the channel needs. Something fresh. And bonus for me—I get to learn from an expert—my idol. This is an incredible opportunity for both of us."

Even in my current sick state, I can tell she sounds like she's interviewing for a job or writing a college essay.

At some point Delancey's going to realize I'm missing. I picture them sitting in the security booth at the fair, answering questions carefully. Maybe they'll first talk to a security guard, and he'll radio the mobile police station. Delancey will probably text my mom. With every step, they might all expect to find me somewhere with my phone held up to my face, obliviously recording new content. When will they know to worry about me?

"So the cabin." The girl just chatters on as she drives me

farther and farther away. "I'm sure you have questions. Built in the early 1900s, but Sonny's made a ton of upgrades over the years. We'll definitely have Wi-Fi of some kind up there, even if we need to run it through the satellite.

"I should probably warn you about Sonny." I feel my whole face involuntarily flinch. "No, no. You don't need to worry about Sonny. He hasn't made his way up to Packwood for years. There's no way he's headed there anytime soon. This time of year, we might see a few leaf peepers. Even that's doubtful."

They'll comb the fairgrounds first, still expecting to find me sitting at a lone corner table with hands sticky with cotton candy and my phone with a useless dead battery—just another dumb, lost kid.

"Sonny's cabin is way out there in the foothills of Mount Rainier. The way I figure it, we'll get out there, get settled, and start cranking out content. If we wrap up early enough before the pass closes for the first snowfall, then great. If not, we'll spend the winter up there."

She's talking about the winter. The truck pitches over a rise in the road and a fresh wave of nausea washes over me. This girl, Nora, hasn't taken me away for a night or two. She's not going to drive me home tomorrow and let me out of her truck in the fair parking lot.

I don't know a whole lot about the mountain. We don't ski. I've gone there on school trips. And of course, in Tacoma, the mountain watches over everything we do. Sometimes you lie on the beach or sit at a waterfront café and you'll look up to see the snowcapped mountain taking up a whole corner of the sky. Or you drive across the Narrows or up Route 705 and the mountain waits patiently. Pull into the Target parking lot; there's Mount Rainier.

Mostly Mom and I have stayed in the city. We drive to Seattle and camp in state parks along the coast. Just hearing about Stevens Pass makes me nervous. The whole point of the pass is that sometimes you can't. The snow rolls in and that road is no longer an option. My sedated brain scrambles to keep up with the details. I try to file the little remnant of information away somewhere. It's the last weekend of the state fair—late September. How much longer before the pass closes? How much time do I have left for someone to come find me?

Nora chatters as she drives. "I don't mind telling you, I'm a bit of a planner. I'm not boastful either, but you might just be impressed when you see what I've set up for us. I don't want you to worry about logistics at all. That will give your creativity free rein. I've got all the practicalities covered, even if we end up staying through the winter. That's one upside of watching Sonny prepare for World War III for the past few years. We have so many supplies. That's something else about me that I think you'll learn, Shea. One of my core beliefs is that it's important to find the positive side of every situation."

I squeeze my eyes shut, mostly to try to block out her voice for just a few seconds. My head aches; my wrist hurts. My throat burns like I've scraped it raw with the screams I've swallowed, sitting here with my hands tied in front of me. The girl beside me driving the truck just keeps chirping. She's like a fire alarm, low on batteries. She's now moved on to a detailed explanation of the generator set up at her father's remote cabin in the mountains. I feel myself losing myself. Whatever she gave me wraps around me like cotton and softens the sharp edges of my anger. I feel only resignation. I float above the truck's cab. My face presses against the cold window as I try to bring myself around, reminding myself to fight harder.

The road stretches out ahead of us, totally dark and mostly empty. Every now and then, an eighteen-wheeler barrels past us. Loggers making their way down the mountain. I half-heartedly hope the cargo will tumble out across the road, just to watch the girl beside me find the bright side of the crush of lumber. Every cab looks opaque in the darkness. No one can see me with my face pressed to the window, and anyway, I can't even control my face enough to pronounce the word *help*.

She says, "You have no idea, I've been turning it over in my head for months. I've seen you really struggling, Shea." Then she abruptly stops talking. I roll my head toward her to see what's distracted her. She's watching me closely. "This might be too soon. Maybe I have this habit of being too honest with other people. But that's a way of building trust. I hope you learn that as soon as possible. I will always be honest with you." Her voice catches, as if she's choking back tears. "I'm feeling emotional now." The truck speeds up to the next curve. I try to arrange my face into a sympathetic expression. For possibly the first time all night, Nora sounds guilty. "Maybe earlier, I wasn't operating from a place of complete honesty."

With one eye half open, I watch her argue with herself. "I did try my best." She nods. "I worked to build a connection before offering anything critical." She nods again. "It's true that the technical aspects of your videos have significantly stepped up." She inhales and then rolls back her shoulders as if she's working up the courage to say something. "But the content of your channel has suffered." Her speech speeds up, in a rush to explain herself. "I say that out of complete loyalty. I'm a true fan—an early follower. But your heart isn't really in it lately, and all of us can tell.

"You're lucky, you know. You have fans who care so much about you. It would be far easier to just hit unfollow.

"So maybe that feedback is tough to hear. I appreciate your listening with such an open mind. Because I think there's an opportunity here to infuse your channel with a new and fresh perspective. You and me, Shea Davison. Look at us." Nora gestures to our bodies. "Anyone can clearly see a resemblance. But we're also so different. I'm what's next, completely undiscovered. All those folks calling you a sellout in the comments? One quick stroke and you silence them. You make yourself relatable again. You just need to unveil your secret weapon." I look up at her, searching. "Me!"

Nora pounds the steering wheel with excitement. "And if I had any doubts or any hesitations that this was the right path for both of us, well, that was just a lack of belief in myself. And let me tell you, that lack has evaporated. Because I did all of it, Shea Davison. Six months ago, I was afraid to leave my dad's bunker. But I traveled all the way here. On my own. I found you. I . . . well, I convinced you. And now I'm driving us to a place completely off the grid, where we will rely on ourselves."

She reaches for the radio then and twists the knob. "I'm not hurt or anything by your lack of enthusiasm. You're feeling numb from the injection, I'm sure. The truth is, I shouldn't be talking your ear off. I should focus on these winding roads. And you should stop fighting the medicine, Shea. Just put your head back and let yourself rest."

My arms feel too heavy to lift, so I can't wipe the snot off my own face. It's a wet mess with drool and tears mixed in too. Outside the car window, I see nothing but pine trees—a tall gauntlet standing guard on either side of the highway. There aren't any more landmarks to remember. No chance for help has materialized. It's hope that I relinquish when I finally let my eyes fully close. I finally let myself sleep. For the first time, I obey.

When I wake, my wrists still throb, but this pain feels different. It takes some time to understand that I'm not sitting upright in a truck. Now my body stretches across a mattress. The silver band of a set of handcuffs encircles my left wrist. The other cuff is locked around the headboard of the four-poster bed. The metal digs into my sore skin and my shoulder aches and feels lopsided and dislocated.

"Help me, please. Somebody, help me!"

I croak the words. I try to boost myself up but my arm gives out from under me.

"Of course I will. I'm here to help."

It hurts to turn but I force myself to confirm she's real. The girl from the maze of mirrors sits cross-legged on a shabby armchair next to my bed.

"You don't need to shout, Shea. I'm right beside you."

"Somebody, please. Somebody, please help me!" With all the strength I have left, I lift myself off the bed, trying to get more air in my lungs.

"Listen, I know you were kind of out of it last night, but I worry that you didn't pay attention to a single thing I told you. That's just rude. That kind of behavior reinforces the stereotype that influencers are self-absorbed."

The fog in my brain dissolves slightly. "Nora," I pant.

"Good. Better."

"Nora. My arms are killing me. I think I'm really injured."

"Probably. I did my best, but you didn't fully cooperate. Then getting you from the truck through the front door—that was an ordeal. You got pretty banged up in the process. But before you passed out, we chatted for a good long while. Do you remember any of it?"

"You took me—" I pause to catch my breath, and Nora purses her lips. "To your father's cabin." She nods encouragingly. "In the middle of nowhere."

"Well, it's not *nowhere*. But it *is* isolated—and that gives us a chance to focus on our collaboration. Remember? We talked about how lonely you were these past few months, all those signals you buried in your videos. I was the only one watching closely enough to understand them. And I'm here now. We're here together. Shea, you don't need to be alone anymore."

She leans forward, smiling widely. I can't stop my body from shuddering in response.

"All I want to be is alone," I whisper.

Nora stands and reaches down. I cower back into the mattress. But she only brushes off her knees as if I somehow carried dirt into the house. "Sure. I'll leave you alone." She locks her eyes on mine. "We'll see how that works out for you, Shea Davison."

CHAPTER 9

NORA

Back when we set the table each night for dinner and argued over whose bath towel was whose, my mom read me books about children who lived in train cars. Helen loved the series first when she was a little kid. So sometimes when my mom was too tired or later when she was too sick, Helen would relent and read to me on the sofa.

I listened and understood that for me, the books would be different than they were for my sister because of the memories that surrounded them. For her, those books were a set of shiny hardcovers she read with a flashlight under the covers. For me, they would stay tethered to the sadness of my mom lying sick in the dark room, of my teenage sister burning grilled cheese for our lonely supper.

And then my mom died, as we knew she would. And Helen moved away, which left me feeling surprised and my father feeling betrayed. Soon after I started calling him Sonny, the way my grandma did. There wasn't a conversation about this, just an abrupt change in how my sister and I addressed a man who seemed to no longer have the capacity to parent.

Anyway, when Sonny first came riding up the road to the ranch with a shipping container loaded on a forklift, I thought of those books about the children who live in train cars. Sonny bought one for himself and one for me. That's how I would explain his style of love—he bought me a separate steel box to live in. Alone.

Sonny says that in the future, we'll all live in containers so that we can move easily. He says we'll need to mobilize quickly to chase more stabilized climates. He says he's advantaged us, that our old ramshackle farmhouse will buckle with the first flood. Sonny believes we'll have to weather high-powered storms and possibly military invasions, once our enemies see our weakened infra-structure. He didn't think of it himself—there's a whole network of men arranging shipping containers around their property like tuna cans in a pantry.

He talks to them—those other men preparing for a disastrous future—all hours of the day and night. Mostly online, in chat rooms and comment threads. A few on his cell phone, but often in a weird code, because they believe the government can tap into cell signals.

I suppose they count as a support network. United in fear and simmering rage. They are always a signal or keystroke away from one another. Because Sonny is always with them, I am always left by myself. Sonny and his friends send photos and vid-eos to one another to compare their full cellars. They teach each other how to dig wells and assemble weapon caches. They talk a lot of politics. Sonny has very strong opinions about politics. He's mapped out detailed diagrams that explain the corrupt forces that have infiltrated our country. He posts the diagrams online for his "friends" to see.

The neighbors who first checked in on us all backed away. The only proof they exist are the Tupperware and casserole dishes we never returned.

I knew better than to complain.

I tried to get used to being alone. Weeks could go by with me seeing hardly anyone besides Sonny. Days would go by without him speaking to me.

In the Boxcar books, part of the fun is how the children live on their own. Those kids don't answer to anyone. No one scolds or punishes them. They take care of themselves and each other.

Sometimes, I hear Sonny ranting. Everything is suspicious, counterfeit, and ruinous. The shipping container children experience independence differently. We have to find our own ways to connect to the world.

I homeschool. Mostly I watch YouTube videos, TikTok, and Instagram. Always I am staring at someone else's life through the tiny screen of my phone or the slightly larger screen of my dad's old laptop. The platforms work like a maze of mirrors. One channel leads to another. You find your way from one influencer to someone else. They create collabs and shout-outs.

Shea outshines all of them.

She's what gets me through.

CHAPTER 10
SHEA

I try to picture my bedroom.

When we designed it, Mom let me pick four different colors for the walls, so I chose light blue, lavender, rosy pink, and mint green. It's a perfect room for TikTok. Automatically, it gives me four different backdrops. I don't love the blue with my skin tone, so I draped a curtain of twinkle lights on that side.

The first few videos, I just aimed for likes and shares. It didn't really occur to me to wonder who might be watching. It turns out my dad was, or at least his lawyers were. They've filed motions and now injunctions. Not out of worry for me, but because he doesn't like how I characterize him. Dad's lawyers used the word *demonizing*. Mom called that a setback for demons.

I try not to think about that.

I try to think about dancing.

I remember working on a dance to an old U2 song. It's

65

fast and catchy and the chorus repeats with just the right ris-ing energy for the kind of sequences I choreograph best. I've got on stirrups, leg warmers, and a sweatband. I look like a vintage eighties ad. My pastel leotard pops against my mint-green wall.

Even with such an intense song, I keep my video light and fun. I wrap up the final chorus with a pirouette that lasts a strong seven rotations and make sure to beam out a smile when I land in second position just as the music stops.

Certain details push into the edges of my memory. Like how I know I made sure my phone was off before wandering out from my room to get myself a glass of cold water. If my room is technicolor, the rest of our house once looked washed in black and white. In those hard days anyway. My mom would leave clothes piled on every surface. The kitchen counters were a sea of discarded containers and empty cardboard boxes.

No one could blame my mom. She did as much as she could. Some days that was a low bar. She would hear me padding softly down the carpeted hallway and call out, "Shea? Are you rehears-ing? Do you want to show me your dance?"

"You can see it later," I'd tell my mom, and then slip back in the refuge of my carefully designed room. I'd switch the angle of my ring light so that it gave my mint-green set a bright glow. I'd stretch a little and then record a video that I knew my mom and I would watch together on a day when she felt stronger. Our heads would bend together over my phone. My mom would squeal at the song choice and point out my strong turns.

I visualize my body as a generator. It powers up. With every motion, every step, it creates energy that I can pass to my mom, my followers, anyone who needs a boost to reach a place where life seems more manageable. I try to radiate joy and hope. Maybe my mom's fog of sadness, before she met Bryan, counted as impenetrable, but I danced to break through that.

My muscles pulse and my toes spring from the special floor that Mom helped me install. By the time I get to the closing set of spins and turns, my smile shines genuinely. I nail the pirouettes and throw my arms up triumphantly as the last bars of Bono's song fade out. I let myself fall to bounce back on the bed. Then I pop up again to close with an extra split. It's just the sound of my satisfied panting that wraps up the video. I stop recording and lower my body down in an elated stretch. It's one of my best videos yet.

Chained to this bed, I try to summon that exact feeling.

I can't quite reach the memory. I open my eyes, half expecting to see my rainbow walls, my gauzy bed. Instead, I find the raw wood of the log cabin. My body is now stretched and strained for other reasons. My arm yanks back and the metal cuts into my wrist. For a moment, the pain stops me from breathing. The beamed ceiling above me spins. It looks like a boomerang filter.

I started recording TikTok videos before Mom allowed me to stay in the house alone. We joked that everything scared me back then; I would never have let her leave anyway. In the long hours of my first rehearsals and posts, I'd pause the music in my room. My mother's low snores and muffled sniffles reassured me.

Now I listen carefully and hear nothing. The woods around me stay silent: no traffic from a nearby road, not even birdsong. The wooden logs of the cabin's walls look like they close in each time I wriggle in the rickety bed. They smother me. I can hardly breathe. My wounded wrist kills me.

"Help me," I gasp out. Then I manage a guttural "Help." I moan and scream and call for anyone. Even if it's only her—the girl from last night. Otherwise, it's just me alone in the silent woods, attached to a bed, no one near for miles. "Please, Nora, if you can hear me, please help me."

CHAPTER 11

NORA

It must be amazing to move through the world and not worry about bothering other people. To be enveloped by the silent woods, resting in bed, and still feel entitled to moan and shriek so that neighbors miles away might hear you. Joke's on Shea Davison, because no one lives within a good forty miles of us out here. She can carry on as much as she wants.

That's a lot of hostility rising in my chest. I force myself to pause and take a deep breath. I inhale and count each of my fingers, exhale and count each of my fingers. Just like the therapist Helen hired taught me to do. Shea Davison doesn't know any better. She doesn't understand all I've put into planning. Celebrity has spoiled her. Shea Davison needs this retreat.

I've intercepted her from becoming a useless influencer just in time. It's a natural development, after all. Someone spends that much time staring into a reflective surface, polishing their appearance, and editing their own image, their worldview shrinks. They only see themselves. Not even themselves—the fake Instagram version they've cultivated for likes and followers.

I've arranged time for Shea and me to step back, to connect with nature, to remember what we love about dance, and to grow a little as a team.

The therapist would point out that I need to accept the ways that yesterday did not live up to my expectations. I'm grieving the image of Shea that I held up as some kind of unrealistic standard. I did prepare for that, though; I understood she wouldn't be exactly the same.

You can see it easily if you study her videos the way I have. Her mannerisms adjust slightly; the way she speaks to her followers has shifted. It used to feel like Shea was talking one-on-one to me alone, like she was a friend on FaceTime or recording a video to lift me up from the gloom of Sonny's bunker.

More and more she sounds like a teacher in front of a classroom. She lectures, she goes on about wellness and resilience as if she's ever survived anything more than a power outage on International Dance Day. The more the number of followers listed in the corner of her channel has risen, the less relatable Shea has grown.

Her venom surprised me. The way she spoke to me as if I don't matter. That took me aback. Her dismissal.

But people react to change in all sorts of ways. I know that. Right now, Shea Davison may not deserve my devotion, but I value my own ability to look past that. If I let her get to me, if I take her shortcomings personally, then I'm relinquishing my own power. And I've put so much work into this retreat.

Besides, I believe that Shea Davison will come around. So I breathe in again, count fingers, breathe out. I do my best to tune out the ruckus she's causing in her bedroom. I turn my attention back to the studio.

It's almost exactly how I pictured. It took a few trips to Home Depot. At first, I went about it too literally trying to re-create the exact colors that Shea uses for her video. But without paint names, it was impossible. Knowing Shea now, I understand that if Behr or Benjamin Moore or whoever had given her a promotional cut, she would have shared out the shades. But she seems to think that her backdrops are somehow emblematic of her channel, as if she's the first teenage girl to enthusiastically embrace pastel colors.

After a few attempts, I realized I was going about it all wrong. The goal was a studio for a new chapter in Shea's journey. Exact replicas of her background would just invite comparisons. They wouldn't inspire growth.

Not to mention, I needed a way to create a smooth back-drop. The log cabin would look like a log cabin, no matter what color paint I used. That's where all those trips wandering around the paint section of Home Depot paid off. Because I discovered canvas drop cloths, and canvas drop cloths are game-changing.

So I made some choices. I painted one cloth a pale yellow

and one a light turquoise. I went with a pink maybe a few shades darker than the one Shea used. She's going to miss the mint green. But I used that color on the studio floor. When we film our footwork, that will provide a terrific callback to Shea's earlier performances.

I'm pretty sure I ordered the exact same strand lights; everyone uses those. They don't count as trademark Shea Davison or anything. I also found reams of cotton batting to create some interest. Between those elements and the two ring lights, I don't see what else Shea could possibly wish for in a mobile studio.

It takes me three trips to carry the drop cloths and the rest of the supplies from Sonny's truck. I climb onto the small cupboard and drill two hooks into the cabin walls. It would be easier work for two, but I can't trust Shea to contribute yet. Besides, I want the reveal to feel special for both of us. Maybe that's an opportunity to turn things around between us. She'll see how much care I've taken in creating a space for her work.

Another way to restore the spirit is through good food. Shea's racket continues, but I don't let it distract me. One flick of the kitchen transistor radio and instead I hear some boy band from the sixties crooning about California girls. She needs nourishment. I fold my arms in front of me the way I've seen my sister do, head cocked to listen to the ungrateful screams of someone who should just settle down and rest.

Then I open a can of tomato soup and pour it in a small pot. I take out the cast-iron pan and butter two cheese sandwiches for grilling. The cabin's kitchen isn't spectacular, but it should serve our purposes, provided Shea doesn't expect anything too elaborate.

The issue of medicine stresses me out. The way she's still howling, Shea must be in serious pain. No doubt she's compounded her injury by tugging so stubbornly at those handcuffs, but I don't want her to suffer, for goodness' sake.

Pills are tricky, though. I don't know how to make someone my size swallow a pill. I've seen Helen give the boys cold syrup plenty of times, however. And I'm prepared. I understood there would be a risk of injury during transport.

If I've done the math correctly, then forty milligrams of children's ibuprofen should at least take the edge off. I heat the kettle and make some instant apple cider and mix the medicine in with it. She doesn't even realize she's so spoiled.

"Please, Nora, help me." Her voice scratches against the wooden door of the back bedroom like an animal wearing down its talons. *Look at that*, I think to myself. *Shea Davison remembers my name.*

I carry the tray gingerly because soup is hot and first impressions are important. Today is an opportunity for a fresh slate.

The tray would please anyone. Tomato soup and grilled cheese is a crowd pleaser. I've included the mug of hot cider and even a napkin. The tray weighs heavily in my hands and the steam from the hot liquids rises to my face. The therapist would tell me, *You can't control someone else's actions, but you can control your reactions.* That's what I repeat to myself as I bump the bedroom door open with my knee.

Shea half crouches in the bed, with her arm twisted in an ugly direction. Her hair's matted on one side and her face is streaked with tears. She'd been mid-scream when I opened the door. Now her mouth hangs open, panting.

"Hey there," I say. "You've gotten yourself really worked up." I approach carefully, because you never know how people will react in unique situations. "You okay?"

"No, I am not okay. I am handcuffed to a bed. My arm—it's really hurt. You need to let me go now. Listen, Nora—it's Nora, right? I won't say anything to anyone. You don't even need to drive me all the way back to Puyallup, you can just uncuff me. I can walk to a busy road. I can call my mom to pick me up. Hey, Nora, by any chance did you pick up my cell phone? When I met you at the fair? Could I get that back? I need to call my mom now."

Clearly, Shea Davison has watched the same episodes of *Criminal Minds* that I have. She's talking very fast but hitting all the crucial points: using my name, establishing rapport, mentioning her mom, appearing nonthreatening, and finally describing an easy de-escalation plan that does not involve the authorities.

I ignore it all and say, "I brought you some grilled cheese and tomato soup—a classic menu choice for building back strength." My hands shake despite themselves and the dishes rattle on the tray. It annoys me; this isn't the time to act all starstruck. I set the tray on the desk and pull the desk over just a bit so that Shea can reach it from the bed. She doesn't seem to fully appreciate how I'm considering every detail of her comfort.

She says, "That's so kind of you, Nora, but I need to get home."

"There's also a mug of hot apple cider. Between that and the bowl of soup, I'm hoping lunch will really cut through this chill. It's colder up in the mountains. You might need to get used to the damp."

"Nora, you seem familiar to me. Have we met before?"

I remember how intimidated I felt at the dance studio. Back then I couldn't even make eye contact with Shea—my nerves interfered with everything. It felt like I'd tilted my whole life to align with her orbit and she doesn't even have a clear memory of that meeting. *It's to be expected*, I remind myself. *I'm certainly going to matter to her now.*

"Your lunch will get cold—all this chitchat. We'll have lots of time to talk, but right now you need to keep your strength up." I shake my finger at her. "And you need to stop bending and pulling that wrist. You could do some serious damage, Shea."

"My wrist is really swollen, and these cuffs are cutting off the circulation."

"That's why you should drink the cider," I instruct. She looks up quizzically. "There's children's ibuprofen in it."

"You spiked the apple cider?" There's the petulant influencer, right under the surface.

"I wouldn't use that phrase, no. *Spiked* implies sneaking; I just told you about it."

"You didn't when you first brought in the tray." Shea's already slipping—she's stopped using my name. She's being needlessly argumentative. The behavioral unit would not be impressed.

"Ibuprofen is an anti-inflammatory. It will help with the swelling. And the pain."

"You could uncuff me." She remembers her manners and her mind games. "Nora, please just uncuff me. My arm—it hurts a lot. I'm worried it could be really injured."

"Oh, it's injured, all right. You stuck it right in front of the door as I closed it."

"Well, gosh, I'm sorry I was so clumsy while you were kidnapping me."

I refuse to engage with snarkiness. "Let's make sure we're clear about the situation, *Shea*. We're at least ninety miles from any hospital or medical clinic. If we have emergencies, we're expected to handle them ourselves. You keep rubbing that wrist, thinking somehow you're graceful enough to dance your way out of a set of regulation handcuffs? I'd guess we have three days before infection sets in. Here's what that will feel like: Your wrist will feel hot all around the wound. Then you'll see streaks radiating onto the skin surrounding it. If we let infection fester, then yes, you can expect to experience some nerve damage. But I figure that's the least of it. If I were you, I'd be more worried about gangrene. Do you know what gangrene is?"

"I've heard of it." The bluster's blown out of her voice. Shea sounds scared again.

I refuse to let up. "Your skin *rots*. At some point, the only treatment option is amputation."

I watch her eyes move around the room. They take in all the details. They search for an exit. She moves ever so slightly, but the handcuffs give her away. They stretch taut, toward the door. The silver metal glints in the light streaming from the window.

I move the desk chair so that it blocks the path between the bed and the door. "I know this is unexpected for you. I've been planning this working retreat for a while, but maybe the surprise has thrown you for a little bit of a loop. I don't want us to get off on the wrong foot—we have a lot to learn from each other."

Shea's eyes well up with tears. "Nora, please." She practically whimpers. "Please just let me go home. No one will know. I'll just show up on a road; I'll say I don't remember anything. Please. People will have started looking for me."

It's weird—when you have someone chained in your country cabin, your feelings veer all over the place. Shea makes me nervous and angry. Her lack of cooperation outrages me. But I feel sorry for her too. She doesn't see her own circumstances very clearly.

"Of course they will have," I tell her. "People will have organized search parties by now. Because you're their meal ticket, right? All those Shea Davison promotional tie-ins and endorsements. But you have to know they don't actually care about you. Look at your latest videos. You're not dancing with love and light anymore; you're just cashing checks. I've followed you from the beginning and, Shea, I had to step in. You've been fading in front of all of us."

The tears run down Shea's face now. Apparently, I've struck a nerve. I make my tone more gentle and say, "Let's just make the best of the time we have together. We can talk about the best way to get you back to the main road when it's time. Once we've accomplished our goals and reminded folks back home that maybe they shouldn't drain the life out of you. They shouldn't take you for granted. And in the meantime, goodness! Let's take care of you. Could you at least try to eat a little bit? That way the medicine won't irritate your stomach. And the medicine will help, Shea. Once you start feeling more like yourself, I think you'll see this as a real opportunity."

Her face shudders with a sob but she nods. She gets it. Shea Davison is a true talent and I'm sure she recognizes a chance to develop her craft when she has a modernized log cabin as a unique TikTok setting right in front of her.

"Great. That's just great. Now let's try to avoid pulling at that right arm. If you just sit back in bed, I'll prop the pillow behind you."

Shea follows my directions carefully. She clearly has come to appreciate that I am a detail-oriented planner who looks out for her every interest.

"Well done." I applaud everything she does, in the same bright voice that Helen uses with my nephews. "Now I'm just going to set this breakfast tray over your lap. You'll need to use your left hand to eat. The soup might prove challenging but look—I've brought plenty of napkins. And it's still warm! You got it?" She nods. The spoon moves carefully and sloshes just a little. I dab at her chin with her napkin and don't acknowledge when she flinches. "Of course you've got it, you're doing great. Could you drink some of the cider too? It will help with the pain." Her left hand trembles as it sets down the spoon and picks up the mug. "Let me know if I need to reheat anything—that's no trouble at all." But Shea doesn't answer me. She sips the cider carefully. I keep having to snap myself out of it—I know I must be staring, but part of me cannot believe Shea Davison is sitting in front of me, slurping tomato soup and sipping cider. The cup rattles slightly when she returns it to the tray. "Don't forget the sandwich. I'm going to get some salve to rub on your wrist, okay? That will help prevent infection—so important. You just keep eating."

And she does. I almost think it's a trick. I keep waiting for her to slam the mug of cider up into my jaw and make a break for the bedroom door. But Shea Davison sits there in the cabin bedroom calmly, occasionally sniffling but generally eating her grilled cheese and tomato soup. I bring two tubes of ointment over to the opposite bedside. I work to keep my own breathing even.

Sometimes my own nervousness infuriates me.

There's a second, when I move closer to Shea, and stand at the farthest point from the door, that she looks up and stops chewing. She stares at the bedroom door and her eyes dart ever so quickly to her cuffed right arm.

I reach for her hurt arm gently, but she still winces. "This salve has geranium extract in it," I tell her. "And then this one is good old-fashioned Neosporin. Because you can't go wrong with that, right?" She nods and sucks her teeth a little. It must sting.

I examine her raw wrist carefully. It's a furious red and oozes clear liquid. "Looks pretty good," I lie. When she's reduced to an injury I'm caring for, she's not so intimidating. My knees stop knocking and my voice sounds more normal. Shea doesn't seem interested in my burgeoning sense of calm or her own healing progress. She barely looks at the bandage I've wrapped around her arm. Instead she stares listlessly around the room. "Well, we've taken care of your arm and made sure you've had a nutritious start to the day. I think we should aim for a little more rest."

"Could you please just uncuff me? Nora, I'll just sit quietly in bed here. We can talk; we can talk about videos and TikTok."

I don't even bother with an answer. I just shake my head. So disappointing.

I pick up the tray.

"Wait." Her voice sounds panicked, desperate. I don't wait. "Nora, please."

I keep my tone gruff. Shea needs to learn she can't manipulate me. Shea's probably not very used to that.

"Get some rest," I say, closing off the conversation along with the bedroom door. My patient has settled back into her bed. She can't have fallen asleep already, but at least her arm lies flat on the bed and not twisted as if she's trying to wrench it off. I lean back against the door and listen for any telltale rustle. But she stays still in there. Then I go about tidying. I'm holding her plate over the garbage can and about to scrape the crusts of her sandwich into the trash when I realize: Those are Shea Davison's grilled cheese crusts. Her bite marks on the bread.

Like any fangirl worth her salt, I put the crusts in a Tupperware and store them in the refrigerator. As I'm cleaning the dishes, the transistor radio plays softly, and I catch myself humming along with the songs. Chores feel different when you're running a household. Shea's cell phone rests on the counter and vibrates against the Formica like a constant chorus. All those parasites refusing to give her a chance to rest. She has no clue how much she needs me.

If I were to build the Shea Davison Museum, I could display her grilled cheese crusts in a glass case. Her cell phone, however, would definitely be the main attraction. The key to her online kingdom is heavier than my own phone in my hand. It's as if all the people calling and texting Shea lend it more weight. Or maybe the thousands and thousands of pics and reels she's got saved contribute to its heft. Even as I'm holding it, it vibrates and I see a message pop up: *Where are you? Just text. We'll figure all this out.*

Shea uses a mint-green case, of course—that's very on-brand. And, of course, she employs a lock screen. I stand at the shut bedroom door and listen hard. Shea's not sniffling or snoring. She doesn't make any noise at all.

The doorknob squeaks as I turn it. When I push the door itself open, the wood groans against its hinge. None of that wakes Shea Davison. She sleeps on her back, with her head curled into her hurt arm. Her other arm rests along her side.

My mother's old quilt covers Shea's legs and tangles around her waist. She sighs in her sleep. Her eyelids flutter.

When I reach for her hand, I feel afraid for reasons I can't name. I worry Shea will wake. And scream. I dislike being startled so I brace myself for her to yelp or yank her hand back. She does none of that.

I hold out her phone and maneuver her thumb to fit onto the screen—just like I watched her unlock it at the studio that night, checking her calendar for the booking note.

The phone's screen lights up. I take a step back and quickly open the settings and reprogram the code. I choose my mom's middle name as a password: Jordan. Strong, solid, and nothing Shea would come near guessing. This is a service I can provide to her—the gift of time away, time to regroup and recover. I know Shea's posting history better than anyone, probably better than her. There's no way Shea rewatches her videos or studies every detail of every post. Not like I do. So I feel more than qualified to step in and post in her stead. I'll keep the channel moving forward in a fresh and compelling way. And maybe new material will slow the deluge of texts and calls rolling in while we're up here at the cabin. Her fans will feel taken care of; her family and friends will see that Shea's just fine.

She whimpers in her sleep and I nearly drop her phone on the wooden planks of the cabin floor. I back up and out of the room quickly. It feels powerful to hold the green Samsung in my hand and have access to Shea's channel with the push of just a few buttons. It also feels like pressure.

I settle on a simple shot. When I hauled her into the cabin, one of her shoes dragged off. I pulled the other off myself and tossed it on top of its mate in the corner of the front room. Now I arrange the sneakers more deliberately. I tie the laces in perfect knots and position the left shoe so that it's balanced on the right.

I add the California filter and a text box: *Ready to dance again soon!* It doesn't qualify as groundbreaking, but it's a start. It buys Shea and me some time as we learn how to support each other, as she learns to trust and rely on me.

CHAPTER 12
SHEA'S PHONE

@ *10:42 a.m.*

> *Snapshot of an oversaturated nature scene: A light*
> *dusting of snow surrounds the trunk of a pine tree.*
> *Dried yellow leaves curl against the tree's visible roots.*
> *The text reads:* On my way to winter, finding
> bright spots.

@ *6:33 p.m.*

> *An aerial shot of a glass vase packed with wildflowers. The*
> *oversized blooms of the deep crimson dahlias look almost*
> *manufactured. The text reads:* Keep your pumpkins.
> These are Dahlia Days.

@ 10:14 p.m.

A quick loop of a hand-hewn rocking chair draped with a patchwork quilt crafted from warm gold and red calicos. The second verse of Dolly Parton's "Eagle When She Flies" plays in the background.

@ 9:02 a.m.

A collage of snow pictures, sepia tinged, with photos focused on elk prints, with the caption Even the elk are dancing . . .

@ 9:54 a.m.

An audio of "The Breakfast Song" plays as the full breakfast tray slides into view. It's loaded up with a full plate of scrambled eggs, cornflake-crusted french toast, and strips of crisp bacon. A green-striped napkin sits fanned next to the food. Then that's covered up with a text sticker: Fueling up for fresh routines. Stay tuned! *The bling-bling effect dissolves the entire image in sparkles.*

The stream of comments scrolls insistently:

Shea! Did you go on vacation? Where is this? Where are you? Shea, reach out. Seriously.

Yum! Looks great! That french toast slaps!

Dolly Parton is a legend—next challenge, Shea? Are you dropping hints?

No offense meant but why does it seem like my aunt Judy took over Shea Davison's TikTok?

Great vacay, Shea! But back to dancing soon?

Shea, please reach out. We need to hear your voice. Give us a quick update.

Looks like Shea's moving to lifestyle content too. You go, Girl Boss. Miss the dancing though!

Where is it snowing, Shea? Alaska? Iceland?

Stop teasing us, Shea! Where you at?

Very quaint? I guess? Does anyone else get the sense that when she finally posts a new dance, Shea will have aged thirty years?

We miss you, Shea! What about Mama Kallie's wedding?

Love Dolly! Love you, Shea! Ultimate collab?!?

Where are you, Shea? We are worried—please get in touch.

Love the new content. How about dorm room design?

Shea, please. Where are you?

CHAPTER 13

SHEA

I arrange my wrists deliberately and position my right arm alongside my left so that I can accurately measure the swelling. It's going down, at least. The gash from the metal cuff still gapes a little but the bruising around it has faded to green. It started as a bright violet, then a deep blue.

I think that means I've lain here for days. I try to track how often the light dwindles outside the window or how many meals she delivers on the tray. I think it's eleven meals so far, with dinner still to come tonight.

I never know how Nora will act, what kind of mood will steer her, but I've discovered certain patterns and clues. Like how she opens the door—if she kicks it open, without knocking, she's already angry about something. That means I need to talk fast and agree quickly to whatever she's decided we should accomplish that day. Nora has some sort of schedule, but it's posted in her mind, and it shifts with her moods.

If Nora knocks softly and peeks her head in before fully stepping into the room, then she treats me kindly. She offers a lot in those moments—a phone call later on to my mom, a hot shower. Those promises never materialize, and I've learned the hard way not to ask after them. But, in those moments, Nora intends gentleness.

I've learned by listening. Nora has a sister, I think. Older. Her name is Helen. She seems to live far away and I don't think she knows where we are. I don't think anyone knows where we are. There are no neighbors dropping by, no parents checking up on us like this is the world's worst slumber party.

Sometimes I fall asleep because I'm tired. I feel like I'm performing all the time, acting like the needy friend Nora seems to want to fuss over. I cry a lot; I beg to go home. I try very hard not to make her angry. I navigate those moments like a tiny sailboat, trying not to sink in the crashing waves of Nora's emotions.

Sometimes I fall asleep to escape. I let myself drift away. I have stared at the knotty pine of this bedroom for hours. I still feel sore; my head hurts in some way pretty much all the time. My wrist kills me and the raw skin under the sharp bracelet of the metal cuff feels like is it rotting away. I pretend I'm back home, shut in my own room, with a lock on my door and my mom right down the hall.

Sometimes I only pretend to sleep. When I hear Nora puttering around the cabin, I try my best to fit in stretches. I strain to exercise. I stay ready to fight. I won't let my body just atrophy in this bed.

When the kitchen faucet turns on, I start leg lifts. When the broom swooshes across the floor outside my room, I do crunches.

When she knocks softly on the door, and calls out, "Shea?," I take deep breaths. Inhale, exhale. It can't look like I've been exercising. She sets a mug down on the desk near the door.

"Oh, hi, Nora." I contort my mouth into a fake yawn. "Do you need help cleaning up?" I keep my voice sleepy so that it doesn't sound like I'm angling to be released. Just trying to be a helpful guest as I lounge, handcuffed to the bed.

"That's so sweet, but no, thank you. I have all of it covered. How are you feeling?"

Terrified. Doomed. But I nod vigorously. "Hmmmnnn-hmmmm." I don't want to commit to feeling a certain way until I understand what comes next.

"I brought you some medicine." She gestures over to the mug on the desk.

"Oh, I'm okay. My wrist feels loads better. But that salve has helped a whole lot."

Nora clucks her tongue, the way our school nurse does when she thinks we're faking cramps to get out of a bio test. "I can put some more on. That's great news that it's healing. I knew it would. You just needed to really rest it. Squirming around wasn't helping anything, you know."

I keep my whole body still. My stomach lurches. I hate that I've basically invited her to touch my arm. She retrieves the tube of ointment from the windowsill. "It's funny how the geranium extract works better than the Neosporin, right? All those harsh chemicals and it's the power of plants that heals us. I packed an herbology book with me. You won't believe what we'll have available to us, if we keep a careful eye during hikes."

I keep my gaze fastened on Nora's face. I refuse to glance over at the handcuffs. The salve stings and I bite my lip to stop a whimper from seeping out. My voice is only the slightest bit shaky when I ask, "You'd want us to hike together?"

She says, "Soon enough," in a flat, empty voice that makes me think I'll never step foot out of the cabin again.

I press a little harder. "I would love some fresh air, Nora." I see her shoulders tense—I've pushed too far. She drops my hand and the cuff clanks against the bedframe.

"Fine." Nora bites out the word. "Let me open a window for you." She moves past me with enough force that I feel myself flinch. But she doesn't touch me again. It only feels like she might punch me. Nora moves the mug from the desk to the bedside table, without looking in my direction. "You should drink that." Her voice sounds gruff, and the door slams closed when she exits.

On the first day of my captivity, I might have cried when she left the room. Now I shake it off. It's a routine with a few missteps. Nothing disastrous. I just have to keep trying.

And then I hear a new sound. I hear a second door slam. I hear the footfalls scatter gravel and then the muffled slam of a car door closing. The engine turns over and fires up. I hear the gravel scatter and know Nora's backing the truck down the drive.

A panic tightens around my heart. Nora hasn't left the cabin all week. I can't even imagine where she'd go. She was angry, but I've seen her angrier before. "She's going to come back." When I hear my voice say it, I recognize it as true. It makes no sense to put all the work into creating the perfect hostage hideout and then leave me handcuffed to a bed just because I asked to go hiking. "It's another mind game." I try the words aloud. "She's testing me."

And then in case of some sort of elaborate ruse, I shout loudly toward the kitchen. "Nora! I'm really sorry. Thank you for opening the window."

I listen hard and force myself to breathe. I half expect to hear the truck careen up the drive, the cab door slam. I wait for her to kick open the door and pelt me with grilled cheese sandwiches.

But all I hear is the hum and gurgle of appliances. I hear birds and the rustle of the wind through the trees outside my open window. For the first time in days, I am fully alone.

I stand up and lunge toward the door out of instinct—only to fall to my knees almost immediately. The handcuff yanks the split skin of my wrist. It hurts so much I swallow down vomit. I remind myself to breathe. I regroup.

I try to examine the handcuffs without jostling them. It's like that game Operation, when you have to reach into the board and perform surgery without making a wrong move and triggering a loud buzzer. I move so slightly, tenderly. I hold the cuffs with my good and free hand and pull at them, testing to see if there's any give in the iron railings of the bed.

The bed is built solidly. It's not going to bend; no piece will twist off and free me. I bend my hand into the smallest claw possible and try to ease it through the metal ring but that still doesn't work—even with the freedom to move every which way and try out every angle.

I'm bleeding again. A trickle of blood runs down my arm. Moving around so much must have broken a scab. Nora will see my blood smeared around and know right away that I've tried to free myself. I breathe myself back to calm. I problem-solve, bending my face to my arm and licking it clean.

I force myself to let go of the notion that I can dismantle an iron bed. Unless I want to just sit and wait, wasting any chance to explore my surroundings, I need to reframe my goals. It takes a few minutes to maneuver, but I figure out that I can push the iron bed a little at a time with my one good arm. I shove an inch or two and then creep forward. Shove a little more and follow with my feet. I work carefully to avoid another moment of hand-cuff agony, but I finally reach the window.

The screen seems old; its silver mesh looks dull in spots, as if maybe it's been repaired. I give myself a few moments just breathing in the mountain air. I take care not to push my face against the screen hard, but I want to. The bedroom walls seem to close in. My whole self rages for the space that stretches outside. I inhale and then exhale. I calm myself.

I crane my head and try to get a sense of the landscape. I see a firepit out back, a swing built from an old ski lift.

92

Otherwise, I see pines. Tall lines of pines, one behind the other. Dense—not like someone planted them as a border between neighboring properties, but thick and randomly spaced in the way that forests grow on their own. The cabin came last, I understand. Someone, maybe Nora's dad or his parents, cleared the land enough to build the cabin and carve a driveway from the woods to the road.

I don't see any other roofs through the trees. I don't smell smoke coming from other chimneys. There's no one to hear me scream for help. I try anyway. But there's no one to rescue me from Nora.

I remind myself to keep breathing. It's not exactly new information. The clear view out the window just confirms our isolation. "No news here, Shea." I say it aloud to myself. "Keep gathering information," I chide.

It feels good to hear my own voice—my real voice. Not the act I put on for Nora with the apology built into every inflection. My cultivated lack of threat to keep her calm and a little less crazy. I inhale and exhale and remind myself that every minute Nora's gone counts as an opportunity. "Find something useful," I order myself.

Deep down, I understand she would never just leave my phone on some random shelf in the cabin. But I have to check. It's the only chance worth taking.

I get to work on the slow task of moving the bed in the other direction. I inch away from the window, keeping an eye on all the dust bunnies tumbling across the wood planks for the floor. The iron posts of the bedframe leave faint tracks in the dust. If I stretch my foot, I can smear them with my toe. At least Nora won't be able to trace every movement when she returns and checks in on me.

I memorize the exact mark on the floor where the bed rested and then keep pushing toward the door. This direction feels more dangerous. Before, I felt ready to thank Nora profusely for opening the window, to explain that I'd felt the fresh air would help me feel my best. Not a perfect line, but at least some kind of explanation. At least I could lean on a plan.

Nora would not consider a field trip to the living room acceptable behavior. I know that. I know it so well I need to refocus on my breathing because my knees shake as I creep forward. My head swims with fear.

Each time I lurch ahead and drag the bed along with me, it scrapes against the wood floor in the loudest way imaginable. I hear the scrape and stop, then try to listen past the pounding in my heart. And then finally, I reach the bedroom door.

It takes almost stretching myself into a split to manage swinging open the door with one hand, while my other wrist stays linked to the bed. I end up counting down twice before I can gather the courage to turn the knob and shove the door open. And even as the door swings outward, I prepare myself to see Nora perched on a rocking chair, staring at me, waiting for me to step out of line.

The cabin is empty. I find the kitchen in the corner to my right. I see the front door, but it's not the kind with a window; there's no way to see past it to the front of the house. It looks like Nora has been shoving around furniture herself. A sofa, armchair, and coffee table lean against the wall closest to the kitchen. Someone's painted one long wall of the cabin with four different colors. A curtain of twinkle lights rounds out the collection of backgrounds.

It's exactly how I'd prep the space for videos. At least, if I wanted consistency. Filming outside in front of a stretch of pines would turn a whole new page. But I don't expect Nora to know that. I get the sense she's new at all this.

In the corner, by the front door, I see my shoes. They look like I just stepped right out of them. Without thinking, I step closer; pain signals sweep through my arm. My throat aches too. I feel like weeping, seeing my sneakers there and remembering the last time I kneeled down to tie them tightly. It feels like years have passed since the night of the fair.

My eyes scan the room: shelves, countertops, bookcases. I don't spot my phone anywhere.

She hasn't left much of anything out in the open. I contort my body every which way, trying to locate any advantage. No neighbors, no phone, no weapons. None of the risks I've taken have resulted in anything more than my continued helplessness.

And now I need to put myself back to bed. Just the idea of it threatens to defeat me. I take one last look outside my bedroom door and try to memorize every detail. I promise myself I'll review every mental snapshot of the cabin's layout during the long hours spent sitting around like a houseplant in Nora's care.

I pull at the cuff around my wrist purposefully. The pain snaps me back from moping and I get to work. Slowly I inch the bed back to the exact place it had been. I make sure to line up the bed's sharp angles with the marks left on the bedroom floor. I remind myself that details don't escape me. I'm trained to be exact in my actions.

I look back to my sneakers in the corner and note they had happened to land in third position. Then I remember tiny Shea Davison, who lived in a leotard and snapped to attention every time a dance teacher counted out a beat. This girl Nora, with her swaying moods and her brooding quiet, does scare me.

But I have steadied myself at a barre, while a grown woman paced behind me, slapping a wooden stick against her hand. I've stared at myself in the mirror while Madame Flint announced to the whole room that my talent was questionable and really, I'd been given access to the advanced class due to my unyielding mother. I've leapt into the air while Madame Flint shrieked at me to make my thick thighs work against gravity. I've steeled myself to stand with perfect posture while a volatile woman prodded any soft spot on my body, hissing that I'd need to step up my training, that she could see the exact spot my lunch had landed on my hips.

I know how to respond to pressure with precision. I breathe deeply and recheck every tiny element of my surroundings. I expect to hear the truck come barreling up the drive at any moment, but until I hear those wheels, my body won't allow itself to be folded back into the bed. I move the rest of me as much as possible, even as I keep my left arm carefully still. My muscles relish flexing. I relax a little and let myself enjoy the exercise.

I don't notice my socks until I hear the rumble of the truck approach. I hear the gravel give under the wheels just as I realize that I've been using my stockinged feet to smear any tracks through the dust on the floor. The white cotton that covers the bottoms of my feet is now stained sooty gray.

Of course, Nora will check the bottoms of my feet to make sure I've stayed in bed. She's crazy but she's not stupid. She's managed to set up the cabin just so and orchestrate an elaborate kidnapping. Chances are, Nora would describe herself as detail-oriented too.

The truck's engine chokes off as I desperately tear the dusty socks off my feet. I submerge them in the full mug on my bedside table just as Nora slams the car door shut. Then I hurl the mug onto the floor. It shatters spectacularly. I wipe drips of the liquid off the bedside table with the socks and then drop them onto the small puddle on the floor below me.

I hear footsteps on the porch out front and then the jangle of keys turning in the lock. I inhale and count to four as I exhale. I settle myself back in the bed and pat the cover down around me. I close my eyes and wait for Nora's scrutiny.

CHAPTER 14

NORA

The key sticks in the old lock of the cabin's front door and I try not to panic. An image flashes of my hand turning it too hard or fast and breaking the metal tip in the lock, with Shea Davison inside and me standing here with chili ingredients on the front porch. That cannot happen.

I take a deep breath and force myself to count to three. When I try again, the key turns cleanly. The whole ring jangles as the door opens in front of me.

I have spent most of the afternoon bracing myself as one wave of anxiety crashes over me after another. I agonized about leaving Shea alone in the cabin. Then because I hadn't driven the truck for days, I worried I'd somehow forgotten how. The whole time I ran errands, I listened for sirens, half expecting to see my face on the little TV the guy had going behind the counter at the gas station mini-mart.

Probably, though, it would be Shea's face. Someone would have started looking for Shea long before Sonny thought to wonder where I'd wandered off. At the market, I used cash and then caught myself counting and recounting the bills. It is a finite sum after all, and Shea and I can only work as long as my stash of dollars lasts us.

I calm myself by taking stock of all the good luck tokens I've gathered around me. The keys that I set on the shelf near the front door, Shea's sneakers in the corner, her phone in my pocket. I run my hand across each color on the painted wall and bend to plug in the fairy lights. I make myself drink a full glass of water. Only then do I let myself check on my guest.

I knock softly on the bedroom door; it's so quiet in the cabin. I don't hear Shea sobbing or wailing. Hopefully, that means she's finally getting some solid rest. "Shea?" I open the door as I ask. I pronounce her name like my mom would mine calling up the stairs—sternly but with care. Shea murmurs a little sleep noise.

And then I see the shards of the mug on the floor. "What happened here?" I ask. She grunts a little. My voice gets sharper—more than I mean it to. But that ocean of concern churns again. She could have had a seizure. "Shea, are you all right?"

"Nora, I'm so sorry. You left medicine and it seemed like such a good idea, but then my hand just trembled and shook. I flat-out dropped it. Please tell me that mug wasn't an heirloom."

The worry waters recede again. "The *Greetings from Mount*

Rushmore mug was not an heirloom, no." I peer down. "Are those your socks?"

Shea sighs. "I tried my best to clean it up. The socks were all I had. Because I couldn't grab a paper towel from the kitchen or anything like that."

She's always angling. "There's no need for you to clean anything up. You certainly didn't need to sacrifice your socks." I retrieve them from the sticky puddle. "It gets cold in here."

"I just feel so useless. You've got such an amazing place here, but you're working so hard to take care of us. I could do more to contribute. I could help with chores."

"You can't even lift a mug, Shea. We've got to give you some time to heal and get your strength back. I'll get the broom and dustpan. You just stay put."

I can't name it, but it feels different in the cabin. Tense. Some kind of power has shifted. Helen would tell me to stop approaching the situation from a place of paranoia. She'd say that growing up with Sonny taught us a kind of pattern, but that we could embrace the ability to disrupt that pattern. Helen doesn't fight through the same undertow I do, just to keep my head above the waves that crash over me every time I have to talk to another person.

I focus on the tasks to accomplish and that helps me calm myself. I carry the porcelain fragments to the trash bin and bring back a bowl of soapy water and a sponge. "What a mess." Shea bites her lip dramatically as she watches me scrub.

"Really, don't worry about it. The stain comes right up.

I'll go get you another pair of socks just as soon as I clean up."

"Thanks, Nora." Shea looks like she is weighing what to say next. "My arm is still really sore."

"I'll bring you some more medicine. And we can put some salve on the cut." I don't leave room for Shea to ask about the handcuffs again. I don't leave space for her to request a shower. I operate with a new rule—every time Shea uses my name, I respond with complete frost. She will not manipulate me.

"I'm just not sure all that's helping. Maybe—"

But I cut her off. "Well, next time don't strain to mop up any spills. There's no need for that. You're a guest here." The statement hangs there in the room, but Shea doesn't reach for it. She doesn't comment; she doesn't correct me. "Okay so, medicine, fresh socks, and I sure hope you like chili."

I close the bedroom door behind me to give myself a break. Shea demands so much attention. That's the downside of providing us with such a quiet haven—Shea isn't used to isolation the way I am. But she'll see the benefits once she and I can really start rehearsing and recording.

The excitement starts to rise in my chest as I prep dinner. I chop peppers and slice onions. As I wind up the can opener, I listen for any sound from the bedroom. That's when I hear her snuffling in her room again. Whimpering. I slam the pans on the burners. I cannot believe she's crying again.

Concentrate on the task at hand, I remind myself.

I focus on making a healthy meal—fuel for us. I think of

101

her like a colicky baby. She needs to cry it out. Shea is a creator after all. She's probably restless with lack of expression.

She's also probably experiencing a little bit of withdrawal. If I'm being honest, Shea displays classic symptoms of an addiction to her phone, to social media. Those aren't difficult dots to connect and of course I'd considered it in my planning. But now that I see her suffering through those symptoms, I have a better understanding of the serious nature of her dependence.

This retreat might just turn out to be the best gift I could have given Shea. When I began planning, I didn't fully understand how much she needs this. And maybe her followers need it too.

The whole time I cook, Shea's phone shudders in my front pocket. Tiny waves of alerts lapping against the shore. Thank goodness I switched it to vibrate. Otherwise, the notifications would have driven me to distraction. These interruptions must punctuate her entire life.

What's up with the unplanned vacay? No songs to post, Shea?

We miss you, baby girl.

Shea, please let us know you're okay.

Can't wait to see the new material, Shea. Must be magic to warrant an all-out hiatus!

Shea, any take on Kamalani Enomoto's latest post?

Re: Kamalani's post—did she shut you down? You hiding?

Hey team Enomoto, not everything's about your girl. Shea can take a break if she needs one.

Yah, so can we. Baby girl, your numbers are falling. The people want more than nature photos.

Shea, please post a selfie. Just a quick pic to let us know you're okay.

Re: selfie. Shay's okay, fangirls. She just got tired of Kamalani dancing circles around her, so she turned into a snowy emo tree.

Give us a break, Kamalot—Shea's obviously going through something major. Not the time.

It just goes on and on—a steady stream of commentary and questions. Demands and assumptions. I don't know what Kamalani Enomoto's followers intend to prove. It seems crazy to root for one girl at the expense of another, as if we're horses racing around a track.

But it's clear that in the TikTok arena, Shea is now considered a limping thoroughbred. *Let them write her off*, I think to myself, scraping the burnt beans from the sides of the chili pot.

Shea has me to help her stage her comeback.

CHAPTER 15

SHEA

When Nora comes back, she brings in two bowls of chili. I can tell she's all wound up about it because she brings in some for herself. We're going to share a meal together—me sitting on the bed, Nora sitting in the chair beside me. She grates cheese over my bowl, as if we're at the creepiest restaurant ever. But I play along. I try to make her happy.

"Gosh—you've taken care of all the details! Where did you learn to cook, Nora?"

"My mom taught me. A little bit at least. My sister taught me more after my mom died." She says it matter-of-factly.

"Oh. I'm so sorry. About your mom."

"Yeah. Thanks." She looks up. "It was a while ago."

"And you call your dad 'Sonny,' right?"

Nora shrugs. "I mean, I try not to call him at all."

I don't know where my laugh comes from, but it rises from

a dark place in my heart and bubbles up to the surface. Nora looks up, surprised at my laugh, at her own joke. She grins a little sheepishly. But it counts as an actual moment of connection. She seems legitimately human in that moment.

"I don't talk to my dad either," I offer, reaching for any kind of connection.

Nora says simply, "I know." I don't ask her how. She has probably watched every single one of my videos so closely. She might know me better than most of the kids who see me in school every day.

I try again. "I can't imagine how you feel, with your mom gone. I miss my mom so much." It's a clunky effort, and it lands in the space between us heavily.

Nora examines the food in front of her. She watches me while I try to maneuver the spoon and the bowl with my good hand. My napkin slips off my lap and falls to the floor. She picks it up and tucks it into my shirt—a bib for a blubbering baby.

"Do you ever feel like you're too close to your mom?" Nora asks.

"Yeah. I do."

She nods to herself. It feels like I've passed an honesty test. I don't elaborate, though. Details feel like betrayal. I know my mom is looking for me right at this moment.

Nora sets down her fork. She picks up her glass of water, but she doesn't drink. Instead, Nora turns it around in her hands like she's studying it. "Before my mom died, Sonny was around.

I never thought of him as distant. Strict, maybe. Quiet. But then after, he decided not to be a dad." She states the obvious. "We're not close."

I try to imagine it. "How old were you?"

"Ten."

I suck in my breath before I can stop myself from making a pity sound. But I picture Nora, younger, bewildered by the sudden absence and cold.

I remember sitting at my mom's bedside with a bill that I'd dared open, trying to get her to understand that the company had turned off our heat. I say, "My parents split up and my mom just went to bed. For months. She was sad, not sick." Nora nods. She knows all this. "I started using TikTok, just to feel less alone."

Nora raises her eyebrows. "Did it work?"

"Yeah. It did. And then my mom found her way back. It took a while. But by the time she tuned into the videos and the platform, I needed help managing all the details."

"So then she took over. You built it and she took over." Nora's anger flares up. She's not mad at me, but on my behalf.

"No, that's not how it went. The stuff that my mom does— the booking, the marketing—it doesn't really interest me. She takes care of that now and it frees me up to dance. And to figure out filming. My mom's not some predatory stage mom; she's my biggest supporter."

When Nora starts speaking, her voice sounds soft; she almost pleads with me to understand. "I've worked really hard—I've done all of this"—her voice rises as she waves her arms wildly around the room—"just to support you. You show this unrelenting concern for these people who use you, who profit off you. News flash, Shea; I actually care. I care more than anyone . . ."

She slams her chair back and stands over me. I can hear her breathing heavily. "I know, Nora, I know. I'm so sorry." My words tumble and rearrange themselves, trying to form some kind of cushion between myself and Nora's rage. I reach toward her and the handcuffs faintly clink. Both the sound and the pain make me wince. I brace myself for another tirade.

But Nora's voice goes quiet again. "How do you still not get it?"

"I do get it. I understand how much you support me. I just miss home, Nora. I don't mean it as a slam or a slight. You're so brave and adventurous—accomplishing all of this on your own. You even drive. I can't drive, you know. It would never occur to me to try to drive. My mom and I count on each other so much, maybe too much—I see that now. You've shown me that. But I miss my mom. We have only a few weeks of living by ourselves, you know. With the wedding and all, everything's about to change. So I really appreciate the ways you've taught me to strive for more independence. When I go home, I'm going to work on that. I'll be really clear with my mom on that too."

She moves to the door, and I can't help chasing her with my voice. It's shameful how I beg. "Nora, I have to go home.

Mom's wedding is coming up. You know, I'm choreographing this special dance for it. That's a really important moment for the channel. We've hyped it so much. I think it'll register record views. Nora, maybe you could tell me what you think of the wedding number—the song choice—"

But Nora interrupts me. "Hard truth, Shea: No one our age cares about the second wedding of two forty-five-year-olds. That's just your mom, stealing your clout again."

It almost makes me laugh. I think of Delancey explaining how the dance is a stupid intrusion on the wedding day. Now Nora has decided it represents my mom's imposition on my brand.

All this time I've thought of my followers as people who cared about me. So that meant they also cared about my mom. I thought I was connecting with people all over the world. But really, I was just creating an empty image. A passive portrait for real people to love or hate. Nora doesn't know me. She's just observed curated minutes of my life.

I'm going to find a way to leave this cabin. I don't care if I crawl out. I will wait for my hand to rot off my injured wrist. And when I finally get to leave, I won't ever dance again.

Or I'll shut all the doors and blinds and curtains. I won't record myself or even let another person stand in the room with me unless they sign a written waiver, a nondisclosure agreement. What is my mom doing right at this moment? Has she retreated back to her bed? Are Delancey and Bryan taking care of her?

"That's just not what my mom's like, Nora. I appreciate your concern, though." I pronounce each word carefully. I negotiate generously. "I see your perspective—really, I do. You've just misunderstood us."

"Are you done?" She nods at the bowl in front of me. It's as if I hadn't even spoken. I am not about to win a diplomacy trophy.

"It was really delicious, thank you." But Nora still doesn't say anything as she collects the remnants of our shared meal. When the door slams shut behind her, I work to stifle my sobs. After all, it's no use. It doesn't change anything to cry. Instead, I consider all the ways I'll use the time I once devoted to dancing and recording content for people on the internet who I didn't know.

This brand-new Shea Davison will study martial arts. I'll earn belts and everything. I'll train to split wooden beams with my bare hands. I will lift weights. I'll learn to drive. I will guard my privacy. No one will ever catch me unaware again. And I will never need to be polite to total strangers again.

Outside the blue sky darkens. I've lost another day. No, that's too polite. The Shea who autographs every last program while her friends wait to ride the Tilt-A-Whirl would phrase it that way. The Shea who performs, who tries to please everyone. The honest fact is that another day has been stolen from me. Nora stole another day of my life.

When she raps the bedroom door with her standard three short knocks, I feel more prepared—resolved to reveal less of myself.

My resolution fades fairly quickly when I spot the second

pair of handcuffs in Nora's right hand. I've already opened my mouth to apologize when she digs into the front pocket of her jeans for a tiny silver key.

I shut my mouth, force myself to wait and listen. Sometimes when Nora leans over me, I imagine biting through her throat. She coos at me, "We're going to be super gentle so that we jostle your sore wrist as little as possible. So just take it slow now, Shea." She fastens a second cuff around my arm. She loops the other end around her own wrist in a swift motion that looks practiced. Here I am promising myself to take self-defense classes, but it seems like Nora has gone to kidnapping camp.

Maybe there's a TikTok channel and she has spent hours rehearsing the complicated choreography of captivity. Once the new set of cuffs is secure, Nora takes the key she's pinched in her lips and works it into the first set of handcuffs. She doesn't fumble this part either.

When I'm finally free from the bed, relief doesn't wash over me. There's no flood of optimism. After all, now I'm linked to Nora. I still have a metal ring wearing down the delicate skin on my wrist.

But Nora has given me new information and that sliver of possibility for escape has widened slightly. Now I only need to overpower Nora to find a way to a main road. I'd just need to drag her with me.

I've spent so much time in my own head that I worry I spoke my plan aloud because Nora warns me, "I am much stronger than you. I'm heavier and you're hurt. I know these woods and you don't.

"You know that's not safe. Not for you or me. But listen, you also can't just sit here and wallow. You've got followers who count on you. Right now, they're waiting . . . but honestly, that kind of patience is pretty short-lived. You need to record a new video. And I know—that's stressful, but I'm fully prepared to help."

"What? Nora, no one cares about my videos. Please, just let me go." My voice begs but doesn't even register. Nora just plows forward.

"I have some song choices in mind, but I'm eager to learn more about your process. So maybe we need to start with the music. We can listen to a few different selections. We don't want to go too dramatic here, Shea. That may be tempting, but it's cheap and sensationalistic. I think the rebrand will go more smoothly if you let the performances speak for themselves."

"Wait, you want me to record a video? Like this?"

"Thank goodness I'm here. God, you are sweet but you're clearly contending with some brain fog. Let's work to focus a little bit more. I need you to keep up. When's the last time you went six days without posting?"

My head swims, trying to make sense of the fact that I've been missing for six days.

"Yeah!" Nora almost shouts. "Exactly. I've done my best with just a few visual elements but honestly, it's still very much your channel, and your followers want to hear from you."

"You've been posting? You've been impersonating me?"

Nora's head rears back and the hardness returns to her eyes. "That is not the term I'd use. I have been *representing* you, Shea. And by the way, you are very welcome. If we had posted nothing, if your channel just went silent, how do you think your followers would react?"

I just shake my head. Nora plows forward, practically shouting. I hold my sore wrist, so she can't pull it while waving her arms. "Eventually, they'd unfollow. They'd forget. You'd fade into just another face they sort of remember from their bored browsing. They won't remember your technique or your sad mom. If you disappear, they'll disappear right back."

I feel okay with disappearing. Worrying about followers and shares and likes seems so unimportant now. I can't imagine facing anyone right now, let alone staring into a camera and smiling.

"Can I take a shower at least?" I ask. My voice sounds small and hopeless.

"You haven't earned that trust, Shea. You know that. And frankly, I didn't expect you to be quite so vain." Nora brushes a stray flyaway from my face. "But listen, I'll do your hair and makeup. We'll give you a slicked-back wet style so your hair won't look quite so greasy.

"I know the cuffs aren't ideal. And I'd love to unlock them—we want that wrist to heal without a scar, but you have to realize we're just not there yet. I can't rely on you not to run.

So we'll just have to move carefully. You and me—we'll need to work together, but think of it as rehearsal. We're syncing our bodies. That's just going to come through in the dance later on."

Nora's words land sporadically and I try to file away information as best I can. She plans for us to dance together. My arm might scar. Those details knock my breath loose in my chest, but I work to keep calm.

All I wanted was to be set free from the bed. My arm ached. I used a bucket for a bathroom for six days. But sitting here, now bound completely to Nora, feels so much worse. I feel like a leashed dog, a pet for Nora to control.

"Let's go slow at first. Easy on your arm." She stands up, holding her arm out in front of her. Nora nods to me so I stand on command. We shuffle across the bedroom floor. I am careful to widen my eyes, as if the four-room cabin is a property on *Million Dollar Listing*. I don't want Nora to realize I've already done some exploring on my own.

"The bathroom's right this way. I think we can give up the bucket, if you behave. I'll face the door to give you some privacy."

I want to die. The thought slams into me before I force myself to complete the basic tasks that come with being a human being and not a Labrador retriever tied in someone's yard. When I'm finished, she lets me wash my hands and points to a new toothbrush on the bathroom counter. It's green. Nora made sure to choose my signature color.

She helps me extricate it from the plastic packaging. "I

113

don't have floss. Sorry. You probably have a super conscientious dental routine." I shake my head. "People always comment on your smile. I needed braces, but Sonny was not going near that expense. So I've got this snaggletooth." Nora lifts her lip. "I'm not really worthy of close-ups, I guess."

"My mom doesn't let me whiten professionally. She thinks it's bad for enamel. I use filters. You have a great smile. People appreciate unique features. Your snaggle is super cute."

Nora's face opens up. "That's so kind of you. I can't believe you said that. Shea Davison, thank you so much." If I were a dog, I'd wag my tail. Instead, I just smile and nod. Nora claps her hands together, jerking my arm. "Okay—makeup time. I can't believe we get to build a look together. Do you always do your own? With your hand and all"—she nods at the cuffs—"I think you should let me help you." She says it like I have a choice.

"Yeah, of course. Most times I do it myself. Sometimes a friend helps." I can close my eyes and picture Delancey biting their lip in concentration while I try to hold still. "My mom does it sometimes; a few times we've hired a professional, but we can't really afford to do that all the time."

"Maybe not yet. I've been practicing a lot, though. I think I've gotten pretty good. I can re-create most of your looks."

"Awesome." The one word sounds sarcastic. Nora's head cocks to the side. "Really." I rush to reassure her. "That's going to be such a huge help."

She nods and smiles. "Just wait until you see the full kit.

I spent months putting it together. With samples and sale bin finds. I could launch my own channel, I swear."

"You should seriously consider that, Nora. That's a great idea."

"Right? Can you say *spin-off*? Hey, let's sit over here on the sofa. That way, I can reach you more easily." We awkwardly shuffle into the living room. She carries the plastic makeup case that once in a while bangs on both our knees.

She sits me down on the sofa and then lowers herself down on the table in front of us. "Okay, let's create some magic. This is so exciting—to step behind the scenes. I wonder if we should film part of this. A sneak peek of me living out a fan's dream."

I struggle to keep my expression neutral. She's talking about posting a video. With her in it. Nora's face will be out there, in public, for someone to identify and hopefully trace to this cabin. The possibility stretches out, right there, but if I'm too enthusiastic, she'll see it too.

"You have such a good read on my followers, Nora. Whatever you think is best."

"*Our* followers," she corrects. "But for now, we should keep the focus on you. Give the people what they want to see."

Nora examines my face, creating a plan for my makeup. I can't let even a shimmer of tears gather. I jiggle my foot to try to concentrate on a different part of my body. Every inch of me bristles with her scrutiny.

"Look at you shaking! Are you nervous, Shea?"

"Maybe a little." She's still going to film me, share it publicly. I must look terrible. My eyebrows have grown like thickets, and I haven't properly washed in almost a week. But anything Nora shares has the potential to lead someone to our location.

"We'll tackle your hair first. I'm going to brush in some dry shampoo. That will soak up some of the oil." I love how Nora points out my greasy scalp like it's some kind of indication of my personal hygiene and not caused by being held captive. She treats me gently, but that makes it worse somehow. I wish she would just yank my hair, slap some foundation on me, and call it good.

I sit there and endure. "Close your eyes," she says, and I lower my lids. "Purse your lips." And I do. Nora holds up a handheld mirror when she's done, and I stare into it curiously. I look like an extreme version of me. For one thing, my face looks thin and drawn. My cheeks have hollowed and my skin has dulled. Nora's drawn my eyeliner with a heavier hand than I usually use. The lip gloss she chose is darker. Delancey will notice differences. So will my mom.

"I love it." I turn the mirror this way and that and wonder, if I smashed it, could I use a large shard as a weapon? "Have you picked out a song? Did you have something in mind?" People make requests all the time in comments. I try to convince myself that this is just another time like that.

Nora shakes her head and says, "Aren't you going to do my makeup?" She holds out a sponge and a fistful of products.

"Yeah," I tell her. "Sure. Same look?"

Nora nods and lifts her chin up expectantly. My hand shakes. I think of the mirror. I feel for the tweezers. There's a chance to do something, with Nora's face turned to me and trusting, her eyes shut. But my mind blanks and my hands shake. She opens her eyes to ask, "You sure you got this?"

"Of course."

"You're not used to collaborating much, are you? We have to work on that."

I think back to Delancey and the others, our studio rehearsals. "I'm getting there. I'm still learning. I don't usually do anyone else's makeup." I steady my one free hand and squeeze an eye pencil between my finger and thumb.

"I think it's actually that you're selfish."

Whoa. Nora's come out fighting. "Well, goodness. I'm sorry you feel that way."

"And that's not a real apology. You should take ownership of your actions, Shea. It's just an observation from an unbiased party. You're usually very focused on yourself." Nora's tone is so matter-of-fact. I just sit there, painting her face while she assassinates my character.

"Most times, for me, dancing is a solitary act. It's the way I express myself." Nora's jaw sets hard. I swab at it gently with the sponge. "But of course, I'm open to growing. Especially if that's important to you."

"Good. Because it's important to me." Nora puckers her lips and I paint them carefully. "I think we go back to the eighties.

117

Punk, maybe prog rock selections. Those have been some of your best videos, and that would capitalize on some of the dated decor of the cabin. It'll look like we meant it."

"That sounds great to me. Here, see if this meets your approval." I hold up the mirror. It feels heavy in my hand. Briefly, just for a split second, I imagine rearing the mirror back and swinging it hard, like a baseball bat. Nora's head would snap back. A tooth or two would come flying out. And I'd still be linked to her by a set of metal handcuffs.

Nora stares into her reflection. She wilts a little bit, like she expected to see someone different. "I love it," I tell her. "Your eyes really pop with the angled wing."

Nora just shrugs. "I mean, it's still me. But I appreciate you trying."

Maybe it's the close proximity or because we're starting to feel like mirror images of each other, but I force myself to have a little empathy for a girl with a case of makeup samples and a dead mom. It's clear no one's made a habit of telling Nora she's pretty. While that's not the most important thing, I know how much it matters to be noticed when you feel like the rest of the world has deliberately ignored you.

"You look great, Nora," I reiterate. And then a new thought strikes me. "Let's post a photo just of you. Here, hand me my phone."

"Easy there, Tiger." Nora smiles tightly. "I think you should stop thinking of it as your phone. After all, doesn't it feel so much better to not be tethered to it all the time?" she asks without a shred of irony. I fight to keep my eyes from wandering to the handcuffs. "I even changed the password." There's a warning in Nora's voice. "I just think it's better to avoid temptation." Then she pulls out her own phone and says, "Okay, get ready. Here's the song I've been considering." It's a Cure song with a fast beat and a catchy chorus. It sounds raw in a way that's missing from their later albums.

"Yeah. I hear it. You want to work out some steps?" I stand up without thinking and suck my breath in through my teeth. I expect to see a ribbon of blood unravel on my wrist. "Nora, just for the dance, it'll be so much better if I can move freely."

"Please don't ask again." Her words sound deliberate. "You're an expert. This is just a complication to work around. Be creative. And hey—" Nora stretches forward and reaches for a knit bundle balanced on the sofa's arm. "I made us matching leg warmers."

They are mint green, of course, with an intricate cable knit. "Wow. You really did think of everything."

"Well, I figured for this first video, we'd keep the shots focused on our legs and feet. We'd really keep the audience's attention on the steps. So the leg warmers add interest and create a uniform look. White socks, don't you think? That's to keep it consistent."

My heart plummets. I try to keep my voice even. "Yeah, that's great, but we spent so much time on our makeup. We should start with a low angle, focused on footwork, and then expand the shot on our faces."

I don't add, *So that someone recognizes your face and calls your dad so that he leads the police to his remote cabin.* That is, however, what I mean.

The problem is, I think Nora knows that's what I mean. "Maybe for a later episode," she says. "It's okay for us to do our makeup for ourselves, Shea. Consider it a confidence boost. I think you need it. And I'll freely admit, I need it too."

She grins at me, and I see a shred of something smug and sinister in her expression. Nora knows exactly what I've been counting on, trying to get her face in a video. I tipped my hand, I can tell.

"So let's review." She ticks off the points on her fingers. "We've settled on an early Cure track. Legs and feet only. We're linked at the arms and we're going to stop whining about that. I'll keep up in whatever ways you need, though. It might take me some time to learn but I won't hold you back. I can promise you that, Shea Davison. I've been waiting for this moment."

She is terrible. I mean she's terrible because she kidnapped me and has held me in a rural cabin until I expressed willingness to perform for her like a trained monkey. There's that. But Nora also happens to be a terrible dancer. She moves with a stilted, self-conscious rhythm. Her limbs look like they were screwed on in the wrong positions.

I keep revising the routine. I simplify it to keep my wrist

still and then I streamline it to account for Nora's inability to execute any kind of basic dance move. She apologizes profusely and that just makes it worse because I feel embarrassed for her and sorry for the ways she clearly doesn't believe in herself. At the same time, this appears to be a major detail to overlook. How could Nora have practiced every tiny component of an abduction, but not actually spent time learning basic dance moves?

She makes a misstep and berates herself. Then she reassures me that she's perfectly capable of keeping up. She blames her nerves and the drafty air. She blames the uneven floorboards and the silent pressures she feels from my expectations. She does not blame the fact that we're handcuffed together, which does throw everything out of whack. I reassure her and we restart the music. Only to watch the train wreck in slow motion all over again.

It takes hours to record ninety seconds. I stop whimpering when my wrist jolts against the metal handcuff because then Nora dissolves into another round of apologies and excuses. "Maybe you should just do it," she says at one point. "I mean, if you are going to intentionally arrange a piece that's impossible for an untrained dancer to manage, we might as well just film you."

"You can do this, Nora." I try my best to bolster her confidence. And then because it is a chance and she is unraveling with every take we attempt, I offer up an alternative. "Maybe just let me do it solo once and then you can use the video to practice? You might be right—I don't mean to overcomplicate the choreography. It's going to be awesome to feature you in the dance. And maybe, only if you want, maybe we release the song first with just me. Then for the next post, we break it down with the two of us—like a B side?" I lay the groundwork. I try to stay a step ahead of her.

Nora pants a little, out of breath from all the failed takes. "It just surprises me. I may be self-taught, but I've always been able to learn your routines. This feels like a lot of pressure, though, with you right here, griping about your self-injury. You're just not the best instructor." Nora sighs. I picture pacing behind her and slapping a cane against my palm, the way that Madame Flint always kept the beat.

"I see that. I'll get better at coaching. Should we set up the phone over here or . . ." I can't risk asking Nora to take off the cuffs again.

She puts the phone on record and sets up the timer. It's strange to see her handling my phone with such expertise. "Don't worry," she says sourly. "I'll make sure to keep my amateur self out of the shot."

"I didn't say that, Nora. Really. Try not to get discouraged, okay? I've done a lot of bad sessions. I just don't post those. We'll get this done and then tomorrow you'll make your grand debut. For this one, do you want to just focus the camera on my feet?" I ask as if the answer doesn't matter, as if every sliver of hope doesn't hang in the balance.

"No, you're right. I think we save that angle for the two of us." We both pretend that Nora's not worried about publicly posting her face. "Besides, I did an awesome job on your makeup." She takes a plaid blanket off the sofa and winds it around my arms. It covers the metal ring around my left wrist.

"I guess I'm better at editing videos than starring in them. Shea, don't try anything, okay? I'm going to go through frame by frame. I'll know if you change the choreography."

"Yeah, of course. I'll do it just the same way." I've become an actress as well as a dancer. Pretending I don't know what Nora's implying. And then, acting as if a notion just occurs to me, "I might tone my energy down a little bit, though. That way, when we post our version tomorrow, it'll really slap."

When the music starts and I have the relative freedom to move on my own, I first think of the people who will watch me. Nora will dissect every sequence, so I keep my expression serene. I need to dance through the gate of her gaze without setting off any alarms.

Once she uploads the video, I'll have other eyes on me. Delancey will analyze every glance, every step. My mom will study my posture, my positions. Hopefully, they will notice the fact that I can't really move, since my wrist is attached to another person.

I don't let my lips form the words *Help me*. I focus on the lyrics. I hit each marker on the floor and keep my eyes straight forward. I don't linger on the blanket wrapped around my arms

123

but I'm quick and sharp with my left wrist, hoping to slip a glimpse of metal cuff in the shot or even drip a bit of blood.

I keep my limbs close to my body. I don't go all in on any movement really. And I don't smile widely. I hold back my dance dial to a four. It's not as easy as Nora might think. It helps that I'm in an unfamiliar room, that I hurt, that I hate her.

But then the music seeps in and it feels so gratifying to let myself be swept away. I savor every way my body gets to move. I remember how it once felt to find myself alone and know that I could still dance through it. I hurl myself through space. I turn up the dial.

I picture myself on their little screens, turning in tight circles. I keep my followers' eyes on me. *I still exist,* I want to scream. *Please. See me.*

CHAPTER 16
DELANCEY

"Dad, you really have to see this." I lean in to peer at the tiny screen of my phone and call him in from the kitchen.

The two police officers sitting across from me look away. They both gave me the once-over when they first arrived. I saw the glance between them—the unspoken agreement to be careful with pronouns. Then the cops began to study the house. Granted, most of our guests spend a lot of time taking in the details of my father's design. He's done his best to cultivate serious mountain chalet vibes. The great room, with its stone fireplace, wood beams, and wall of windows, imposes with coziness.

I know Dad has asked the police to meet us here instead of the station. He leaves Kallie alone as seldom as possible. And then there's the fact that his house stands as his ultimate flex.

Earlier, when I called him on playing the rich guy card, my father leaned forward, kept intense eye contact, and told me,

125

"Do I think it's right that Tacoma PD might treat Shea's case more attentively after meeting here? I do not. But you know what, Delancey? You're going to feel more comfortable in your own home than down at the police station. And I've worked very hard for that rich guy card. If I don't flash it now to find Shea, then I don't know what it's good for."

So now the Tacoma PD and I wait, facing one another on artfully weathered leather sofas, while my powerful father arranges a tray of healthy snacks.

His hospitality feels unnecessary. They already seem impressed with the architecture. And still they stare at me like I'm a set of fingerprints showing up on a dusted surface.

"Is this the video that Shea posted earlier?" Detective Agarwal asks, and I lower my eyes to my phone. "We have technicians reviewing that footage. It's good news, right? Shea is dancing again. Hopefully, she's working through some of her issues."

Dad strides in with waters and snacks.

"Much obliged," Officer West says, like he's in a cowboy movie and tying up his horse.

"Shea doesn't have issues." I turn to speak to my father. "Did you watch it really closely? There are a couple of moments in particular when she seems really off."

"Everyone has issues, though, right? I know I do. I bet you do, Delancey?" Cowboy Cop looks down at his notes as if it takes a huge effort to get my name right.

"Excuse me?" Dad puts his ally voice on, and the cop rushes to double back.

"I don't mean anything specific about your child, sir."

"We are happy to follow up and hear Delancey's perspective on your missing stepdaughter." Detective Agarwal speaks slowly and deliberately, looking down at a small notebook as if reading off a script. "Just like Officer West says, we do consider it a positive turn that we're seeing activity on social media initiated by Shea. She's keeping up with her usual habits. It gives us eyes on her. We know she's safe."

"Can you trace the location?" I know my voice sounds impatient. But they sound like followers, not investigators.

"Do you recognize the location at all?" West asks. I shake my head. "We have not yet accessed the considerable resources we'd need to trace these posts." The cops look over to my dad almost apologetically. "I don't mean to upset anyone. But this fits the pattern of a typical runaway situation. The upcoming wedding, an estranged father. A teenager with more independence than most young people her age. We see these family dynamics play out again and again. After a while, you get a sense."

"Shea's only sixteen years old. She can't drive. She's not in contact with her birth father. And there's a lot going on right now. This isn't like her."

Agarwal says, "From what I gather, Shea has cultivated quite an online presence. Could she have met up with someone? Has she been corresponding with anybody in particular? Maybe she asked you to keep a secret, but you see how worried her mom is and then you need to rethink some promises. Does that sound right, Delancey?"

"No, it does not sound right at all. I've been telling you all this since the very first night. We were in the fun house. She vanished. There was no one. She would have told me. We tell each other everything."

Officer West holds his hands up. "Just hear me out, will you? Let's say I'm Shea. I'm an internet star—an influencer— that's the name for it, right? I'm putting myself out there. I'm posting these dances because I love all the attention. So then I disappear—from a public event like the state fair, no less. Seems like lots of people click on me then, right? That kind of mystery comes with lots of clicks."

My dad presses his lips together, the way he does when he's striving for patience. "That's not the kind of exposure Shea pursues. She keeps really careful boundaries with her online presence. And Delancey does not keep secrets. We have a very open and supportive relationship so that I can properly advocate for my child."

I am done striving for patience. "We're wasting so much time with all this. What are you saying—you think this is some kind of publicity stunt? We haven't heard from Shea for six days." Dad reaches over and places a hand on my arm—his signal for *Tone it down. Remember who you're talking to.*

Officer West points out, "But we *have* heard from her. Shea *has* posted images. And now a video. It seems to me that she's communicating quite clearly. I know that's hard to accept. Oftentimes in these situations, giving some space helps defuse the tension. She'll come home when she is ready."

I look from my dad to each of the police officers. "You're not listening. I thought you wanted to interview me because you understood how well I know Shea? She wouldn't just disappear." I shake my dad's hand off my arm. "You're getting married in three weeks. Do you really think Shea would do this to you and her mom?"

He sighs heavily. "I'm trying to consider all the possibilities." I don't know where I lost him. Dad turns to the officers and tells them apologetically, "We do have some complicated dynamics. Blended families present challenges."

I tap on the screen of my phone again and hit replay. Tiny Shea starts dancing again. She moves listlessly and barely smiles. My dad shifts his stance again. He reminds me of one of those giant windsocks at the car dealerships. He blows one way and then the other. He tells the officers, "I gotta say, Shea doesn't look healthy here. If nothing else, she needs a wellness check. Can you at least do that? Trace the location and then just stop by and check on her?"

"Where is Shea's mom?" West asks. "Is she available to talk?"

Dad and I sit very still. Above us, Kallie lies closed in her darkened room. I have not heard her speak since I showed her the video. She let out an animal sound, a keening wail that first made me believe that I missed something in the footage. It sounded like Kallie had seen Shea's body, not her diminished dancing to an old eighties song.

"She's not available right now." My dad's voice is firmer than his shifting allegiances. "She's resting."

"I could go get her," I volunteer. "Then you can tell her it's fine that you don't know where her teenage daughter is. Since we have a video in which Shea looks exhausted and starved, you're pretty sure that's just a stunt."

"Okay, now, Delancey." Dad issues a verbal warning.

Officer West leans back in his chair and lets out a slow whistle. "You're pretty angry about all this."

"Someone took Shea. She was abducted. People are counting on her. She wouldn't just disappear." I swing my words like a hammer, hoping to break through.

But Officer West just shakes his head sadly at me. "We see this differently. I see someone who maybe needed a bit of a break. Sir, neither you nor the girl's mother has given us any reason to suspect she was being threatened. We have no notes, no reports of stalkers, no break-ins or vandalism." He turns to me then. "Delancey, I'm glad that you don't have experience with the pattern, but typically when teens are kidnapped, they're not spending their time posting photographs of plants and snowfalls."

I hit replay again and watch Shea lean forward and line up her steps with the beat. She twists and whirls but doesn't execute a full spin. She moves stiffly, and then loosens up her limbs as the song continues. Almost ninety seconds in, Shea's smile cracks through the impassive wall of her face. Recognizing her in that moment just underscores the absence of her spirit earlier.

Dad leans forward and presses his hands against his knees. "You don't know Shea. That makes this hard. I'm glad we can see that she's alive. But Delancey's right to say she doesn't look like herself. She's a kid. She shouldn't be out on her own. And I'm not law enforcement, but that suggests to me that Shea might be in danger. I do sincerely hope you're right. But God help you if you're wrong."

My father moves to stand up and the officers look relieved to be free of us. And right at that moment my phone chimes. "Shea has posted another video," I read excitedly off the screen.

Officer West looks over at his partner. "Well, what do you know?" It feels strange to crowd around my phone with two cops and my dad, waiting to see my best friend's latest TikTok video. I want her to be okay, but if she isn't, I hope Shea makes her predicament obvious. I hope she gives me something to show them.

It's more 1980s glam—the Cure, I think. It opens with a peppy keyboard. I see a set of legs. Pretty sure those are Shea's. She's wearing gray leggings and green knit leg warmers.

"It's just her legs?" Dad asks.

"Can you make it bigger? So we can see all of her?"

"That's not how it works," I try to explain. "This is the shot."

"Is that some kind of trend right now?" Officer West asks. "Showing just half a person?"

"No," I tell him. The four of us watch breathlessly as Shea's legs stomp and turn and then another set joins her to dance in unison.

"Who's that?" Detective Agarwal asks.

"We don't know who that is. Because it's just half of a person."

"Presumably a different person," he answers with authority.

"Right. Because Shea does not have four legs." The second dancer wears matching leg warmers over black leggings. It may be an odd choice of aesthetic, but it's a fun style—the cropped shot makes the viewer focus more closely on the movement of the legs. Without the distraction of facial expressions or arm motions, our eyes zero in on steps, stomps, and kicks. Even the leg warmers work to Shea's advantage—they outline the shape of her muscles.

"Well, there you go," West says. "It looks like she's staying with a friend. A dance friend? Does that sound right?"

"It doesn't sound right," I insist. "She still doesn't show her face. After the last few videos, that just keeps up all the weirdness. Plus, I know all her dance friends—none of them have seen her."

"I agree with Delancey," Dad says. "This doesn't necessarily confirm that Shea is okay. She could be hiding an injury."

"Or she could be ensuring that locals don't recognize her," West says. "Maybe she's protecting the identity of her friend. I don't see a conflict here. They're dancing together."

"Well, they're both dancing." The policemen take a few steps back; my dad holds my arm as if to reassure me. I try to explain, "It's almost impossible to dance with Shea. I get it—you think these are just silly kid videos, but she's a classically trained ballerina. If you watch closely, you see it."

The video has ended without ever expanding to include the dancers' faces. The camera never drifts upward to include anything else. "Just watch again—one more time. You'll see that this person dances a lot differently. You can tell who Shea is."

I hit replay. The two pairs of legs moving in unison are a cool effect, but the truth is the setup works to the other dancer's detriment. Shea's motions flow from one sequence to the next. Her grace seems effortless. Next to her, the other pair of legs strains at every step. That dancer doesn't stumble, but they do lurch a little. They step cautiously while Shea moves deliberately.

It's impossible to look anything but clumsy, moving alongside Shea. I know that because I've tried to dance next to her.

Detective Agarwal's not having it. "We can't just go around arresting people for bad dancing." He swings his head to face my dad. "This is just not an investigative thread we will follow."

Officer West looks down at me with pity. "Listen, Delancey, it's really hard when friendships change. Especially in this case, you two are pretty much family. But that just proves you'll be close no matter what."

"My friendship with Shea hasn't changed." My voice sounds so bratty, even to me. "We don't know where she is. Her mom doesn't know where she is. This video doesn't prove that Shea's okay."

"It shows her dancing." There's a sharper edge to Agarwal's voice now. He's not feeling the same patience. "We've got two teenagers, wearing matching clothing, posting dance videos. Mr. Renard, if you want a trace, I will apply for a trace. But Tacoma PD doesn't take responsibility for interrupting unsanctioned slumber parties."

"I understand, gentlemen." Dad sighs heavily and rubs his beard with his palms. "Listen, this is just so out of character. Let me talk with Shea's mom. But I know we want the trace. It's not a priority, I get that. We still have a child who's missing, though, and we need to know where she is. Then we'll do what we need to do to bring Shea home and address it as a family. Thanks for your time. We appreciate it."

West nods, mollified. I stand there and fume while the two officers file out the door.

When my dad returns to the living room, the house feels different. He stands on one side and I'm left on the other. I'm replaying the latest video on my phone. On my laptop, I scour the lyrics for clues. I have a notebook out to jot down notes. If the police won't help Shea, then I need to figure out where she is. We haven't gone this long without contact since we met in second grade. If she posted a video, I'm sure that she has buried a message for me in there.

Dad clears his throat. "Before we talk theories—are we okay?"

"I don't even know what that means." I sound petulant but also accurate. I don't understand who counts as *we* anymore. The definition of *okay* appears out of reach too.

But I can't help asking, "What are your theories?"

"Well, I just have the sense that before I came on the scene, Shea shouldered a lot of caretaking on her own. She cared for her mom during a serious depression. That's a lot of pressure. And maybe now that I'm here, Shea feels more able to step away and focus on herself. So she's spending time with a new friend. She may be rebelling—something she never had room to do before."

"I don't think that's happening here."

"Okay, but can you acknowledge that maybe it's a possibility? A less dramatic possibility?" Shea dances in the square screen I hold in my hands. *What is happening, Shea? Why hide your face? What are you protecting me from seeing?*

I force myself to breathe. I remind my father with my most even and calm voice, "Here's what happened. We met up with friends at the fair. No one argued or stormed off or texted passive aggressive comments on the group chat. I went into the fun house and when I came out, my best friend was gone. Diana, Pearl, Jolie, Marcus, and I searched everywhere. Then we called Kallie. Kallie called the police and they basically shut down the fairgrounds. I'm not being dramatic."

"I know, I know." My dad has his *no offense* hands up—his usual stance when he's about to be offensive. "That was an incredibly traumatic experience for you—and not at all what I believe Shea intended."

I fight to keep my breathing steady, to not flip the coffee table or throw one of my father's architecturally interesting decorative objects against the wall of his great room. He says, "I'm just looking out for you, kiddo." I know he really means it. My dad gazes at me reassuringly, believing he's scoring parenting points all over the place. "We might not reach an agreement right this minute. However, if you're currently feeling centered and solid, I'm going to head upstairs and try to talk through some of this with Kallie."

I watch him climb the stairs. His voice sounds so positive, but his head bows forward. His hand is braced on the banister like he's desperate for support. It feels disloyal because Kallie has treated me with such unswerving kindness, but I want to run past him and drag her out of bed. *You've used up your right to retreat,* I want to tell her. *Fight for your kid. Storm the police station. Shout something.*

Shea's house is smaller than my dad's sprawling showcase property. When I visited, I couldn't help but see the ways her mom had withdrawn, how she'd left Shea to fend for herself. I remember taking off my shoes when I arrived, not because Shea and her mom worried about dirty floors, but because they made our footfalls heavier, and Shea tried her best to let her mom sleep through her days.

I know Kallie to be so kind. And I know Kallie to need so much. Chiefly from the two people I care about most.

When the police arrived, they banged on our carved wooden door the way the police bang on doors in the movies: forcefully.

I'd been waiting for them to arrive, and the sound still jarred me. All that commotion, how could Kallie not come rocketing down the steps, wide-eyed and waiting for news of her daughter? How could she not be sitting with her finger on the refresh button every minute of the day since the first post appeared on Shea's channel?

Maybe Kallie would have scrambled out of bed if it was a talent agent or a recruiter for a Netflix dance competition. The ugliness of my own thought sets me back. I sit down on one of the kitchen stools and just let it wash over me. Who have we become? Kallie petrified in her bed upstairs, my dad bro-ing it up with the cops, and then me, alone in the kitchen tasting my own rage and hoping neither my dad nor Kallie can read my mind.

Somewhere, Shea is out there. If she's dancing and recording, then she's counting on me to see every detail. I hit play for what feels like the thousandth time. There must be some detail, some hidden message that I'm not seeing in these two latest videos.

Above me, the floorboards creak. At first, I'm hopeful. Maybe Dad has rallied Kallie, maybe they'll both come downstairs. We will solve this as a new and offbeat version of family. Blended, like Dad says. Not shaken.

But that's not what happens. The cavernous house settles around me. Outside, the wind whips up from the waterfront.

It's hard for me to close out of the app. It feels like abandoning Shea. But then I start texting and messaging. I give our friends two hours to meet me. Six days and Tacoma PD still has nothing. The only leads that exist are those posts showing up on Shea's TikTok.

I know some experts in Shea's channel, though. So I do what I need to do.

I summon her top followers.

CHAPTER 17

NORA'S PHONE

The view counts on the two videos of "Close to Me" keep rising and the comments roll in.

Most tilt positive.

> *Dance4life331: There she is! Welcome back, Shea.*
>
> *LunagirlfromlLA: Shea, you okay, girl? We missed you.*
>
> *CalistaEmory: Love the '80s vibe, Shea.*

Every once in a while the creep factor sneaks up:

> *DavidRunner: You like Robert Smith? I'm an old sad man. How about me?*
>
> *TechassRose: I'd like to get close to you, Shea.*

And then the insidious comments—the slams that arrive under the cover of raves.

Mimi1999: Shea, you've slimmed down. Those cheekbones slay.

GirlGemNYC: My mom loves the Cure. Maybe next time, a more current choice?

CaDANCE: Love the raw and messy look, Shea. Not aiming for perfection looks good on you.

Second video get more hits and more chatter.

TechassRose: Huh. Not sure what to make of this. All okay in Shea city?

MiloDennehy: I know, right? Shea, show your face.

GunzKnivesKnitting: Who's the new set of legs?

CaDANCE: Keep practicing maybe? Though I love seeing the unpolished steps.

GirlGemNYC: This feels a little off-brand. Whattup Shea?

Devo, using a robot avatar and very little punctuation, comments on every single post. Each entry expresses a different measure of disbelief.

Shea, you okay? Send up a signal if you need help.

Shea, we love and miss you. This seems out of character.

Hey, Shea fans, if you're alarmed and think this is off-brand or unexpected contact your local law enforcement.

That comment disappears within minutes, right after garnering its own controversial responses.

> *Seriously, Devo? Call the cops on awkward TikToks.*
> *We don't endorse swatting.*
> *Devo=Drama*

Notifications keep chiming on Nora's phone. And they're not all for Shea's TikTok. Texts pile up. The ones from Helen go left unread.

> *Nora, honey—how's the visit? Are you sure you shared all the details with Sonny?*
> *Nora, you missed your appointment. You promised! Pick up the phone. Let's talk this out.*
> *Nora, please reach out to me. Confused about where you are. Help me help you!*
> *Did you seriously take Sonny's truck? Nora, what are you playing at?!?!?! Tell me where you are.*

Shaky fingers turn the sound on Nora's phone down. The phone keeps blinking with each notification.

CHAPTER 18
SHEA

The wind picks up with enough strength to make the electricity flicker. Sitting on the plaid sofa, linked to Nora, I'm seriously yearning for the good old days of isolation in the back bedroom of the cabin. At least then I didn't feel obliged to make conversation. It's as if Nora and I have been assigned to be partners on some terrible school trip.

What's worse is that *she* doesn't seem to mind sitting here beside me for hours. I'm not arrogant. I appreciate my fans. But it's unnerving to notice the unhealthy obsession of the person sitting beside you and realize that the object of their obsession is you.

The lights blink again, and I imagine how much worse this situation will be if I have to sit here next to Nora in the dark.

I must flinch because she says, "You don't need to worry. The wind won't knock the power out. We have a generator."

"Oh yeah, everything seems really sturdy." I laugh a little, like the idea we would lose power in this tiny tinderbox of a house is absurd. Who would think of that? "So your dad built this cabin?"

"Yeah. Sonny built it with his own dad. More than fifty years ago. I think my granddad figured they'd develop this whole side of the mountain. He wanted to get in early. But then the state put in an easement to block the loggers. And the county had trouble with the dam. Anyway, it's just us really. For miles . . ."

I file away the details: the mountain, the easement, the dam. Eventually, something has to prove useful. I search for something to offer, to keep Nora talking. "Delancey's dad built their house. It's on the water so the winds from the sound can be murder on the internet. But you seem to have great connectivity." Nora doesn't comment. I try another angle. "Delancey's my friend—"

"I know who Delancey is." Nora sounds annoyed now. "I follow your TikTok, Shea. Delancey's dad is going to be your stepdad." And then she fires off, "I've met Delancey."

"When did you meet Delancey?" It's shimmering in front of me—a gold filament of hope. I resist the urge to snatch it up and keep my voice measured, uninterested. If Delancey has met Nora, then Delancey will remember Nora. They're so much better at tracking all of that than me.

Then Nora says, "The same day I met you."

I feel dizzy. The room pitches sideways as if Nora and I are sitting on a ship and an enormous wave has rolled under us. Steady, steady.

"We met? You mean before the night of the fair?" The

memory of Nora in the fun house is still shaky, wobbly from both the layers of mirrors and whatever she injected me with.

"Yeah. We did meet before the fair. We had a conversation. Of course you don't remember. You were so focused on yourself and the dance for your mom's wedding."

I risk her rage when I tell her, "I'm so sorry. Lately, I've had so much going on. I get distracted. I see that now."

"God, Shea. You're insufferable sometimes. You're not saving the world, you know? No one's dying if you don't post a dance video. None of you had anything to say to me at the studio that day. You could not have been bothered. You move through the world tracking your posts and your likes and you never listen. You never notice other people. You gather followers; you don't grow friendships. Delancey's your best friend but all I saw were the two of you sniping at each other. You didn't even listen then."

I am listening now. And remembering. The blurry picture finally comes into focus, and I see Nora now, standing in the corner of the studio. Nervous and never making eye contact.

"You're the dancer we double-booked with. I'm sorry—"

"We didn't double-book. I found you there. I never reserved space at the studio. You would have known that if you'd paid for your rehearsal session rather than take advantage of a freebie."

"Wait—do you know Madison? Did you meet her? Believe me, she wants us to use the studio. Maybe that sounds obnoxious. I can understand that. But they give over the space knowing we attract other dancers to the studio. It's good for their business; it's good for us. That's just how it works."

"That's how it works when you encourage followers. Not when you and your entourage sneer at less experienced dancers. Then you're just like every other powerful person, lording influence over the people you consider lesser."

That is why I sit shackled in an isolated cabin on the side of Mount Rainier. I was snobby. I dismissed someone. I made a person who admired me feel small and inconsequential.

"I'm really sorry, Nora. I didn't mean to do that at all. You are a wonderful dancer, and you know how to direct phenomenal videos too! So much of TikTok is luck—what catches on and gains traction. I shouldn't have forgotten. I've just been so stressed out about the wedding and the changes it's bringing to my family. I know on the site it's all about my mom's fairy-tale ending, but really it's not that simple. It's hard not to feel like I wasn't enough. Just me, for my mom. Now there's not a single corner of my life that isn't complicated." I keep rambling, trying to win over Nora. Somehow I wander into the truth.

Nora still has her face turned away from mine. She stares at the wall, maybe counting up slights, computing what a terrible person I am. But I see her listening. I go on, "And you know, I really wanted to thank you for getting me away from Tacoma. We hadn't properly met, and I understand I didn't make the best first impression. But you still brought me to this beautiful cabin. We have the chance to experience this getaway together. It's made me really take inventory, you know? Review what's most important to me."

I watch my words chip away at Nora's stony expression. I try harder to reach the place where she liked me, where she felt desperate for me to like her. "I really needed this break, Nora. Thank you. It's been such a relief to spend time out here with you. Hard at times, yes, but really inspiring. I can't wait to hear more of your ideas. All I've done for weeks is pretend to be thrilled about the wedding."

"You can't be expected to work like that. That's really selfish of your mom," she says. I stop myself from arguing. I won't gain anything from arguing.

"Did Sonny remarry? Is there a new Mrs.—" I begin the sentence, praying that Nora finishes the thought by supplying her own last name.

"No way. Not even close. Sonny doesn't really believe in marriage. He thinks it's an antiquated social contract that won't withstand the next era of humanity."

As soon as I wrap my mind around this whole situation and try to work it to my advantage, Nora throws a curveball. "What new era of humanity?" I ask.

Nora's voice sounds bored. "Sonny believes that we're balanced on the precipice of a new apocalypse."

"Oh gosh—I don't understand." Not for the first time, I look around the cabin nervously, worried that Nora is only one of the dangerous members of her family.

But Nora shrugs. She sighs with baffled exasperation. "I don't understand either. Sonny says people are growing more and more polarized. Coupled with the way the media has desensitized us to violence, we face a new civil war. He says it's compounded by environmental factors, scarcity of resources, huge wealth discrepancies. You know . . . all of that," Nora says as if she expects that I, too, could list the many factors that will contribute to the end of the world. "Anyway, he won't remarry. Which is probably just as well. He's not a kind man."

I consider the way Nora runs so hot and cold, her paranoia and her eagerness to please. "Does he hurt you, Nora?" I ask.

"No," she says. Then she adds, "Sonny would have to notice me to hurt me. I don't even register on his radar." I think of my mom, a silent lump in her bed, listening to reruns of *Law & Order* for days at a time. I remember how it felt to watch my mom come back to life once she and Bryan started dating. How it felt like a miracle just to see her stand at the bathroom mirror, twisting strands of her hair around the curling iron. I know what it means to understand not being enough on my own to keep my mom moving forward.

"This was after your mom died, right?" My voice sounds raw.

Nora meets my eyes. "Yeah. People deal with grief in all different ways."

"But you have a sister. Does she have the same last name as you?" I've overcorrected. My voice sounds hollow and fake.

Nora's nose wrinkles. "That's an odd question. No, Helen's married. She took her husband's name."

"I was just trying to remember. I know Helen's important to you."

Nora shifts. She straightens her posture and swivels toward the bookcase near the kitchen. She keeps both our phones there. I saw her store them earlier. "How do you know anything about Helen? Have you spoken to her?"

"What? No! You've mentioned Helen a few times. That's all. I'm sorry—I guess I just figured she was important to you." My words rush from my mouth. "I've always wanted a sister, an older sister, like Helen. Someone who would look out for me. You know?"

"It's not always like that." Nora speaks quietly. I keep my mouth shut, waiting for her to share more. "When sisters are older, they leave you behind. They can't help it. It's just how growing up works, right? Helen tries her best. She married right out of college and moved down to California. She has her own kids now, you know. But she stays in touch. It's just that on Face-Time, she sees what she wants to see."

"Oh, believe me, I know all about that game." Nora looks at me quizzically; she doesn't quite get it. "It's just like that on Tik-Tok, same as any content online. People want to see the positive because then they don't have to worry."

"Really? You think it's the same? On your channel, you promote a certain image—it's all sunshine and pirouettes."

"That's true," I admit. "But I bet you do the same thing when you talk to Helen. You act all upbeat and you reassure her that everything's just peachy, even if it's not that at all."

Nora chuckles. It's not terrible to hear her laugh. "That's true. I guess it's more similar than I thought. That's awful to think I'm performing for my big sister!"

"Nora, does Helen know that we're here?" I get that Sonny might be an out-of-his-mind prepper, but Nora's big sister sounds kind and normal. She must already be worried. Maybe she's headed up here now. She'll swoop in and uncuff me. She can help me convince Nora that we can both find our way back from this. I look down at my wrist, which is crusted with old blood and now streaked with purple. Maybe Helen knows some basic first aid too. "Did you tell your sister you'd be at the cabin?"

"That doesn't matter. No one's going to bother us up here."

That's exactly what I'm afraid of. But I refuse to panic. There is a Helen—a least I know that much. She sounds like a reasonable enough person who cares about her sister. She'll be missing Nora the same way my people must miss me. I have a whole set of facts to work into the next video—breadcrumbs to drop and leave for someone to trace back to me.

I lean forward, trying to register as many landmarks as possible. But it's pine trees—row after row of tall pines. Swaying a little. "Even with the wind, it's so peaceful here. Every time I look out the window, I almost can't believe the gorgeous scenery. Maybe we can film our next video outside?" I don't have much of a plan, just to get Nora thinking about our next post. Somehow, I need to give viewers a different view of the property.

"Yeah, we can think about that. We haven't used the cabin to

149

its best advantage yet, though. We've got backdrops. I've arranged some really artful lighting. I know I'm new at this, but I want to contribute, Shea. This whole plan was meant to benefit us both."

I've noticed Nora's voice goes shrill when she's trying to convince me of something.

So I nod vigorously. "Oh yeah, I see that now. Look at us, Nora. We're already expanding the channel in new ways, trying new things. Like the last video, with just our legs. That was brilliant! Can I see my phone? I'd love to check for any new viewers. I usually review adds and numbers every three days. We don't want to lose track of that data—it's super useful."

I look toward my phone and back at Nora, but she doesn't react at all. It's like I haven't even spoken. So no phone, then. "I'm sorry—I'm just chattering away. We just felt very separate for those first few days. It feels good to get to know you a little bit."

And here is the really creepy thing: That's not a total lie. Yes, I am angling. As best I can, I try to connect with Nora. I mine every line of conversation for a contribution to my eventual escape. But also, she makes more sense to me now. I understand why she glommed on to my videos. I get why she sees herself in me.

I remind myself that Nora has stolen me from my own life back at home. She has drugged me and dragged me. She has hurt me. When Nora's feelings and sad story start to matter too much to me, I force myself to examine my maimed wrist. I make myself imagine the bracelet of scars that I'll wear when I finally find my way home.

CHAPTER 19
NORA

My wrist hurts in an oddly satisfying way. It's one part I didn't plan for—the need to keep Shea and me linked together. I didn't count on how exhausting all this would be—the constant caretaking required by someone as overindulged as Shea. The ache of my wrist reminds me. Even when we sit still on the couch, the metal scrapes my wrist continuously. I'm sure it's worse for her. She has that freak injury, which, if I'm truthful, was due to carelessness on my part. I panicked so much in those first few hours. But Shea and I have settled into a daily rhythm. We understand each other.

We are more alike than I ever imagined. I have bruises blooming beneath the stainless-steel handcuff. When all this is over, I wonder if I can convince Shea to get matching tattoos. We can find a dainty and intricate design—something we decide on together. By then collaboration will feel reflexive. Right now, Shea and I are still learning.

Sometimes I have these moments when we're sitting beside each other—at the table, on the sofa. I remember dreaming up this whole adventure—how unlikely it all seemed. How impossible. Sitting here, I feel so pleased with myself. I want Shea to ask me: How did she get here? How did I manage to transport her from my dream to the wood-paneled living room?

When I would catch myself feeling lonely, it helped to imagine who I could invite over to the ranch. If I could spend time with anyone, any guest in the world, who would it be? Who would make each day more bearable? It became a game I'd play in the lonely empty days after Helen headed back to California.

Sonny had his voices on the radio. And I had influencers and the tiny window into their lives—my phone. I could step away through that window. I knew by the way he looked at me, Sonny saw me as a nuisance. A reminder.

Silences stretched for days. We dwindled from *How was your day?* to *Pass the salt, please* and from there it was easy to stop bothering.

Working through chores, trying to homeschool, I'd pretend to have someone chatting along with me. Mostly I'd talk to them just in my head. If Sonny heard me washing up at the kitchen sink and babbling to no one at all, he'd holler that I was acting crazy. So I'd whisper. I would just narrate a little, the way you tell your story to yourself as you go ahead and live it.

Shea's channel was different from other TikToks on dance or crafts or financial literacy. I know because I sifted through all of them. Videos played beside me all the time. Mostly those were people who fascinated me, with lives so different. More glamorous. Far-off and amazing.

At first, I believed the same about Shea. She speaks so confidently. And it takes authority to decide your voice is worth being heard. To press record and then act on the belief that your life warrants sharing. I recognized that power in Shea's videos.

But I saw something else too.

Shea never had to shout over the bustle of a busy household. She never got interrupted or surprised. No brother or sister or parent poked their head into her bedroom to ask some stupid question or call her down for dinner. Behind whichever song she'd selected to dance to, Shea's house had a soundtrack of quiet.

I doubt her other followers realized. But I noticed the hushed way she sometimes spoke to us: Someone lived in Shea's house who she didn't want to disturb. I remember how the idea of it slammed into me. You don't see the quiet houses on Netflix. On TV, the parents joke with their kids. They tease or lecture. Or yell.

Once I understood how alike we were, I saw Shea's loneliness lurking under every video. I started writing down every mention Shea made of her mom, her dad, her house. If I could figure out the Davisons, maybe I could understand the Monahans. I cataloged the meals Shea made for herself—cereal with milk usually, not enough to fuel a dancer's level of activity. I saw that she only filmed in her room. If she included friends, she made those videos at school, at the coffee shop, even at the grocery store. That was something else: Shea did her own grocery shopping. She bought her own school supplies.

Oh, it all got better. I watched that storyline play out along with the rest of Shea's other followers. Her mom gradually made more appearances in her videos, waving as she floated by the open door of Shea's bedroom. I heard her voice more and more and understood that sometimes she even held the camera.

Shea interviewed her mom about the divorce and even her depression. While they came off as more heavy-handed than I would expect from an influencer of Shea's caliber, I appreciated the effort. Shea and Kallie nobly reminded her followers that divorce was an issue between adults, and parents were responsible for their own emotional well-being. They shared so openly that sometimes I found their happiness obnoxious. Especially on days when I needed to wear headphones to cancel out the sound of Sonny ranting.

It's hard to admit my bitterness. I wanted to root for Shea. I saw the way she tentatively watched her mom fuss over her hair before a date with Bryan. As if neither of them fully trusted life to pivot toward joy so completely.

I wanted to root for them, but their happiness also made me feel lonely. And then came the video of Shea and Delancey. Along with all other followers, I watched them both squeal over the miracle of their separately single parents finding each other on a dating app. Shea's house was never as quiet after that.

I'm not going to claim that Shea Davison needs to suffer for her art; she's not Van Gogh. I understand the limits of Shea's cultural relevance. But the forced march of cheer through her mom's second marriage feels empty and contrived. Shea is better than that.

I can't have been the only follower who missed her vulnerability. That's why I stepped in to help. Shea needed a return to quiet. She needed space—someone to run interference between her and her intrusive friends and demanding family. I can't have been the only follower who missed her old channel, but I was the one who risked everything to restore it. She will see that. Eventually.

It's already so much better than I expected—every single aspect of this plan that once seemed so farfetched now seems natural. Certain things still stress me out: every time Helen texts, for one. Worry tends to wash over me while I fix our meals. Shea often picks at her food, and with our supplies dwindling, we don't have it to waste.

But she has started to appreciate my efforts. She thanks me for the food; she marvels at the cabin's wooded views. She complains about missing home less and less.

People have exploited Shea for years. To acknowledge that calls almost every relationship she has into question. I'd like to think she's starting to understand how much I'm willing to sacrifice to help.

I'm not letting the online comments get to me. Most people

resist change. Shea's followers don't understand the ways we're advancing the channel. We're entering a new phase—a more artistic one. Lots of folks willfully misunderstand art. In the past, Shea hasn't shared the spotlight well. So we're dealing with the ghost of that greed now.

I notice it's a few particular commenters. A couple seem to take issue with Shea's very existence. I just serve as collateral damage. They watch her videos for the sake of hating her videos. It's sport to tear her down. Then there are concern trolls—flooding the stream with suggestions that Shea is somehow in danger or unwell. Devo, in particular, seems in tune with the details of Shea's circumstances. Devo gives off hometown vibes.

I want to ask Shea how she deals with it—the exposure, the onslaught of opinions every time she posts. I practiced dance. I studied set-building by watching videos. No one trains you for vicious feedback. But I can't trust her enough to give away how much those comments hurt me.

"How did you find me?" I don't hear her when she first asks. I am that accustomed to having conversations with Shea in my head. And we've sat in quiet for a good while. She asks again, "Nora? May I please ask you a question? How did you find me?" Her voice bounces around the empty cabin.

It's a good part of our story. I'm ready to share it with her. I whirl around excitedly, and she winces. I've yanked our arms. But Shea shakes it off and nods for me to continue. "Okay. Yeah. Sorry." Suddenly, I feel shy and nervous. But still, I can't stop myself from smiling when I tell her: "*Ten Things I Hate About You*."

"What?" Shea looks flabbergasted.

"I've seen it at least fifty times." Mostly with Helen, piled on the couch in the times before our little planet tilted. My sister loved that movie—its Shakespearean roots, its Heath Ledger dreaminess, the poem at the end. "Have you seen it?"

"I know about it."

"It's a classic."

"It's a rom-com. From the nineties."

"It's an adaptation of *The Taming of the Shrew*. That's a play by Shakespeare."

"About the taming of a woman?"

I don't like Shea's tone. "Well, the play is about marriage. Back then, those alliances focused more on economics. It's definitely dated, but has a strong female lead—"

"Who gets tamed?"

When I practiced this conversation in my head, it never went so sideways. This was supposed to be a bonding moment for us, but Shea has fixated on this one word. "The Shakespeare isn't really the point. I'm telling you about my favorite movie. I used to watch it with Helen. We'd watch it over and over. We could both recite the poem at the end from memory. I can't believe you haven't seen it." I get excited again—anticipating the big reveal, the way she'll see how connected we already are. "It's set at your—"

"At my high school."

Shea finishes my sentence for me, and I don't like that. That ruins the moment. And reveals poor manners. "Well, that's such a big deal. I can't imagine that the movie isn't required viewing when you go there. Just think about that, Shea. I first saw that movie so long ago. Maybe I was seven or eight. Helen and I watched it over and over. She even almost applied to Sarah Lawrence because the girl in the movie went there for college. But anyway, all those scenes we rewatched and memorized. Performed for my mom even. They were set at Stadium High School. In Tacoma, Washington. Your high school."

"The school jokes about it a lot."

"It looks like a castle. You're so lucky to go there." I cringe a little, hearing my own wording. Because she's not exactly attending classes right now.

She doesn't point that out. That counts as progress, I think. Her voice still sounds flat when she tells me, "Yeah, I know. That's cool and all. But inside, it still feels like high school."

I have waited too long to share this with Shea. I just keep spilling out details, thinking she just needs to hear the right one to understand. "Helen and I always thought of *Ten Things* as a Seattle movie, you know? And then I watched all the way through the credits—did you know they put bloopers at the end? Anyway, it listed Stadium High School. That's the magical castle high school."

"Right. I get it."

"And then in October of last year, you posted a dance in front of the building. I recognized the turrets. The following

January, you filmed another video on the football field, the one made iconic by the 'Can't Take My Eyes Off of You' scene. The first video could have been a fluke, a landmark you passed by and viewed as an opportunity. But you seemed comfortable there. I thought you must live in Tacoma. Honestly, I was just so amazed you were from Washington state. Another connection between us. Then the second video confirmed it.

"Once I realized you went to Stadium, the rest was just relatively simple detective work. I found a discussion board all about the city. I posed as a parent moving to the area and wondering about the best schools. Those folks provided me with so much information about Tacoma school zoning.

"It became a sort of treasure hunt, looking for local landmarks—like the park with the lion statues—"

"Wright Park."

"Right. Correct." I laugh. "But you know, I found you so easily. As much as I really enjoyed some of those videos, you might want to consider the safety element. Me, I'd never hurt you." I hold eye contact with Shea, all but daring her to glance down at her wrist, but she stares right back at me. "Because I'm here to help you, to advocate for you. But you know, there are dangerous people roaming around."

Shea nods solemnly. She blinks a lot. It's fascinating to watch her face fight to hold still. We're sitting so closely, facing each other. The corner of her right eye twitches and a slight movement ripples across her lips. I know Shea's face so well—I've spent hours watching it, after all. Now I get to see her right in front of me—all the expressions that flicker across her face. And right this moment, it looks like Shea wants to say something but stops herself.

"I know." I pat her arm. "It's really scary. But that's another element for us to work on together."

"Then you found us at the studio?" Her words come out slowly. I think Shea is still in a bit of shock, imagining what could have gone wrong if it had been someone other than me who tracked her down.

"I planned for this to go so differently." Now that we're talking, really understanding each other, it feels important to explain this to Shea. "You just needed to get to know me. I thought if we just met in person, then of course we would be friends.

"This is probably hard for you to hear, but back in Tacoma, you just weren't living up to the person you promised to be. I'm just one of your followers, right? One of thousands. But I've been rooting for you since the beginning. I pretty much risked everything to help you, so I feel qualified to speak for all your followers—at least the ones who really care about you. We've spent years boosting you, liking you, sending positive comments. I know I never, ever minded. In your videos, you showed such a positive attitude, you always spoke so encouragingly. You broke down the steps for your dances. It was all about the ways we could uplift each other, right, Shea?"

She closes her eyes then. She nods. Deep down, Shea is an honest person. She knows what I'm about to tell her.

"Then I finally met you in person. You were just so cold and aloof. You seemed really closed off to new people. And your friends—honestly, Shea, the whole group behaved monstrously. They closed ranks, but not to protect you—I mean, it was just me, after all. It just seems as if they aimed to protect their ticket."

"Their ticket?"

"To fame, I guess? The way they look at you as a launchpad—how Diana demands you list her as a featured dancer, how Pearl and Jolie make you link their own channels. Doesn't the constant angling gross you out? Maybe that's something we should confront them about—really take a stand? At some point, we should make a video specifically calling out that behavior. We can discuss that later. But I'll make a note of it. Shea, we're coming up with so many incredible ideas. We really need to get recording." She blinks again. Her eyes shimmer, just the slightest bit, with tears.

I go on. "I just expected that you and me—we would have more time to get to know each other. That way, when we eventually came up here, to the cabin, right away you'd recognize it for the opportunity it is. I'm sorry that things got so out of hand that first night."

"You mean the night you took me?" Shea speaks quietly, but her words have that hard edge to them. It's her ingratitude that wears on me. I count out a few breaths, though, and try again. We need to work through these hard moments in order to be strong partners.

So I smooth the faded quilt that covers both our legs. I move very carefully so that I don't disturb Shea or tug at her hurt arm. I speak to her in the relentless positive tone I learned from her. "One day, you and I will both look back on this time and think of it as a rescue, Shea. I truly believe that."

CHAPTER 20

SHEA

We sit facing each other and I try to flatten the expressions of my face the way Nora smooths out the blanket that stretches across our knees. I've danced through injuries before. That's just part of ballet. Stress fractures, labral tears. Hammer toes and black toenails. You have to smile onstage anyway. With Nora now I remind myself to stay composed, to stay positive. Every conversation, every minute I sit here in the front room gives me the chance to know Nora more . . . and then to seize on weaknesses.

I learn to let Nora talk. Nora fills silence. If I don't speak, Nora speaks for me. And when Nora speaks, she reveals details. I will follow those details home.

I need to fight past my anger—at Nora for her ranting plans, at my mom for not yet finding me. At whoever left Nora to fend for herself so that she grew with such a bent comprehension of the world. Mostly, I'm angry at myself. It was careless to post at

Stadium, to film at Wright Park. Those aren't even landmarks; they're icons. They led Nora right to me.

I try not to make a big deal of my wrist, because when Nora starts to feel guilty, she stops wanting to look at me for a little bit. That's when she stashes me in the back bedroom.

"I wish I hadn't treated you so coldly when we met, Nora," I say. It's not a lie, after all. "It wasn't about you." Her jaw sets hard, the way it does when she feels slighted. "I suppose I sensed some of those dynamics you were so smart to notice right away. My friends using me. I knew that deep down." I force the words out of my mouth and hope my delivery is convincing. It helps to follow every lie with a little bit of truth. "Rehearsals can be so frustrating; no one takes them as seriously as I do. I mean, until you."

"Rehearsals are really important," Nora grudgingly agrees. "I don't see how a dancer could not see that. They also play an important part in building a team." She sounds like she's reciting a teamwork handbook she found on the internet.

"Well, that's what I really love about this time with you." The lie in that line flares up so I try to douse it in honesty. "I've never met anyone who considered my posts so carefully. You notice everything." Nora nods, mollified. I ask, "What do you envision for the next video?"

"Well, we should decide that together, right? But maybe something edgy and unexpected. We've got to make a statement to the haters—your artistic choices are your own."

It takes everything in me to keep quiet. To stop myself from asking Nora how I should exercise artistic freedom while handcuffed to another person. That would satisfy me for a second. I'm playing the long game now. So I say, "*Our* artistic choices, Nora." And then I watch her glow.

"Let's go with a Washington band," I offer. And then, before she can suggest it—"Something less obvious than Nirvana. Everyone associates Seattle with Nirvana."

"I know, right? It's so annoying." I realize that Nora will shift in line with most things I say. Except the suggestion to let me go home or unlock the handcuffs—she won't agree to those. But I can sway most decisions just by racing to share my opinion first. Nora desperately wants us to operate in harmony.

"So then who else? Someone older, you know? Grungy but not tired? Not Soundgarden, not Sleater-Kinney . . ."

"Alice in Chains?" Nora proposes it, apparently oblivious to the inherent irony. I fight the urge to hop up to celebrate, to congratulate myself on leading her right there.

Instead I congratulate her. "Nora, that's perfect. Such a great idea. I had no clue you had such killer taste in music. You have the whole nineties vibe dialed in, don't you?"

I swear she blushes. "I always stole Helen's music."

"Your sister's really punk rock, huh?"

"Well, now she's a housewife. So maybe not so much anymore. But I used to love riding in her car because then she'd get to pick the music."

"Well, I love Alice in Chains—it's also a little dark and wild, so we can do something different than my channel normally does. I think that's an ideal follow-up to the last one—but what do you think?"

"It might not be the safest choice." Nora bites her lip, weighing factors. "I didn't know how much to tell you."

"Okay. What is it?" I fight my rising sense of panic. What if Nora got my account banned? What if Nora's just posting these videos on her own channel? "You know if we're going to work effectively as a team, you should share the burden of worry with me. You can't just leave me the stuff of choosing songs and looks. You already do so much to take care of me, Nora."

That's the key that unlocks her. "I hope it's not a major setback," she says. "Not everyone liked the latest posts. It might be me. I'm the new element, after all. But to be frank, you're just not looking your best right now either."

Ouch. Thanks for the honest assessment. But I say, "I'm not worried. We're creating something entirely original, right? We already said that. At first, it's going to cost followers. But we just need to keep creating amazing content. They'll flock back."

"Do you really mean that?"

Of course I mean that. I don't need 900,000+ followers anymore. I need one follower, one with keen observation skills who's willing to dial 9-1-1.

But I tell her, "You said the same thing before, right? Listen, when we get discouraged, we need to build each other up.

You've had great ideas, Nora. What are you thinking next?"

"Maybe a call-and-response kind of thing?"

"Like a conversation in dance?"

"Exactly. We can pick the song, divide the lyrics. Keep our style similar but focus on different movements." Nora learns fast. She understands if she follows the same movements, then viewers will compare us brutally.

"I love it, but then we have to show our differences too. We need to make each line of dialogue clear. The last video worked so well because of those amazing leg warmers you knit. That way our legs looked like matching pairs. This time . . ." I drift off, as if I can't quite put my thoughts into words.

"This time we need to look like opposites!" Nora announces triumphantly, and I look at her as if she's just discovered plutonium.

"You're brilliant. I love it. Can we look through your makeup kit again?"

"Yeah, yeah, of course. Right now?" She glances at our wrists, and I consider asking. But then I watch Nora decide not to risk unfastening us. I won't press yet. I'll save the request for a better time with more trust established between us. My newfound patience would astound Delancey.

When Nora opens up the cosmetic case, I take a quick stock of what's available. All the palettes and highlighters are terrific, but I'm eyeing the tweezers, searching for anything else with a sharp edge. Slim pickings. Nora combs through the tiny bottles, sifting and sorting. "I'm thinking geometric eyes."

I have no idea what that even means, but I say, "Exactly," and Nora sputters and giggles like a doll I just wound up. "Does Helen have a favorite Alice song? We could dedicate the video to her or even ask her to do an intro. I know she's in California, but she could record a video and we could splice it together." Anything to get Nora to clue an adult into our presence up here at the cabin, especially before winter rolls in and we face the first serious snowfall.

Nora reacts like I asked for the key to the cuffs. "Well, that obviously can't happen."

"Helen just sounds so cool."

"Helen can't know we're up here. She might not tell Sonny, but she'd come get us herself. And either way, everything we hope for during this time together would go unaccomplished."

"She'd drive here? All the way from California?"

"Listen, let it go. We can't include Helen. We shouldn't want to include anyone. These performances are supposed to be focused on us."

"Sorry, Nora." My voice drips with hurt. "Just thinking out loud." She doesn't quite settle down, so I toss in a sniffle. "I'm so sorry."

"It's okay, but stop about Helen already. It's like me saying we should ask your mom to film an intro—it's all kinds of complicated." My heart slams against my ribs. I think about my mom picking up the phone and hearing Nora's voice. The lilt of her hello, the puzzlement as she sorted out the request, and then how her voice would rise when she figured out who she was talking to. I feel my arms trembling. And I know that Nora must feel my arms trembling, given that our arms are now connected.

She doesn't mention it. It's a small and unexpected mercy. She gives me a moment to gather myself, then switches the topic back to music. "Hey, given that we're aiming for opposite makeup looks, should we go with 'Love, Hate, Love'?"

"I'm not sure that I remember that one. Is it really dark? I think we should steer clear of the darkest tracks."

"I'll get my phone." We're better now at orchestrating the rise from the sofa and the slow shuffle around the living room. I've learned how to hold my hand so that my wrist doesn't bother the rest of me.

Nora pulls up the song, using her own phone instead of mine. It's another detail for me to file away, just in case it turns out useful. We sit there and listen to a few bars and we both shake our heads. We keep listening, but I ask, "It's pretty dark. Too much, right?"

"Way too much . . ." Nora leans forward and grins. "I can only imagine the comments rolling in."

"How about this one—it's better known. More likely that people will make the Pacific Northwest connection." I point to the album art for "Would?" and Nora hits play. It's dark too, but it's got a great bass line and a lyric I can use for my purposes.

"I guess." Nora's not completely sold.

"Yeah. I don't think it's quite perfect either." I keep my voice casual, so Nora doesn't sense how much the song choice matters. "We can regroup. We don't even have to post every day, right? I mean, there's no need to keep up with my previous pace and professionalism. We're doing this differently now."

That gets Nora where it hurts. I watch her stew for a few seconds and then she issues her edict. "You know what? I think we just go with this choice. Think of it as an exercise in letting go of your perfectionism. Right? Doesn't that feel great?"

I make myself hesitate, knowing that Nora needs to believe she convinced me. "Yeah, I mean, no. It doesn't feel great. But I can live with it."

We decide to fully embrace the ragged darkness of the song and go heavy on the eye makeup and flannel. "It makes your grunginess look intentional," Nora snarks, and I swallow my response. I stay focused. We switch out the backdrop and just go with the cabin's dark wood walls with a few strands of twinkle lights snaking down on either side.

I stand there beside Nora and take in the whole look. "What do you think?"

I can hear the hope in her voice. "It's okay."

"Just okay."

"I don't want to fight."

"We won't fight." I sigh and chew the inside of my lip as if I am really mulling it over.

"Shea, just say it."

"You're going to be mad."

"I won't. I promise."

"It's these." I lift my wrist ever so slightly and her hand rises too. Nora starts to glower so I talk faster. "It's just that this is a new kind of music for me to dance to. I actually think it's fantastic ballet music, you know?" I play the part of the impassioned dancer who wants only to serve the music. "But I worry if we're bolted like this, we'll both be compromised. I won't dance my best. I can't imagine you'll dance your best. No one could."

"It really does inhibit me. Some of the commenters called my movement stilted, and I'm sure that's why," Nora says. "I just worry if I give over to the music, it feels like I could really hurt you."

"Of course. I get that completely."

Nora sighs. "I've actually been putting a lot of thought into it."

"You have?" The surprise in my voice is sincere.

"Of course I have. But we're not talking about this, Shea. You could really get yourself in trouble here." Nora's voice suddenly sounds lower and almost programmed in a strange way. There are moments when Nora really scares me. This is one of them. It's not her words so much as the way she delivers them, as if she's worried about me. She acts like I might upset some malevolent force. But Nora is the malevolent force.

I play along. What else can I do? Nora has set it up so that she needs to be both my collaborator and my captor. I defer, I agree, I fawn. "Of course, Nora. Whatever you think is best."

"I think we need to take a break." She speaks decisively. No asking me. I step backward toward the sofa, but she says, "You should rest."

"No, I don't need to, Nora, really. Please." When I leave here, when I'm able to crawl on my hands and knees down the mountain home, I never want to hear my own voice say the word *please* again. I am so tired of hearing my pitiful voice beg. "We can just sit down. Please."

"No, it's time for us to take a break. I have some tasks to take care of. It'll be okay, Shea." She speaks to me the way you speak to a wild horse being led to a stall.

"I thought we were going to record. We both need to finish our makeup. We can sit in the living room for a few minutes if you need to relax." I hate how my voice whines and begs, but I have this unshakable feeling: If I step into that back bedroom, I will never leave it.

Nora does not offer other options. She does not need to push or shove. She just walks purposefully; the raw wound on my wrist makes me an easy follower. The other set of metal handcuffs remains fastened to the iron four-poster bed. We stand there, still close to each other. I try not to feel hurt by this person whom I rationally understand is crazy, whose regard I accept should not matter.

At the beginning of freshman year, my school took us up to Mount Baker for a wilderness trip. The guides from Alpine Ascents taught us to rappel. I remember how we made sure the second carabiner was hooked and ready before unhooking the first and hollering out, "Belay on!" like we were skimming down Everest.

That's what I think of now, as Nora hooks me to one metal apparatus before she frees me from another. "Really, Shea," she says in her calming tone, "try not to upset yourself." Because that's the problem with this kidnapping, I keep upsetting myself. I feel unmoored. I feel like I am plummeting.

I let myself fall back into the white sheets like they are snow-banks, and I will myself to freeze and feel nothing. Nora brings me hot cider a few minutes later. The drink scalds my throat and blanks my mind.

I drift over the lyrics to "Would?" and try to highlight key phrases. My feet circle in the air, practicing. I try to climb out of the deep crevasse of darkness that opens when I am alone in this room. I rattle at the metal on my wrist—both to hear the clanging sound and to feel the wrenching pain. Both prove I still exist. "You okay, Shea?" Nora calls out. "Do you need anything?"

"No, I'm just great." But I say it in a whisper. I feel like that dog in the burning house meme—*this is fine.* I remind myself that it's a relief to have some breathing space from Nora, to have time off from fake smiles and forced enthusiasm. Even though I miss conversation with another human being, the sound of another person moving about the room. I miss the distraction. It's not that I miss Nora but that I've grown used to her following so closely by my side.

I close my eyes and give myself over to the darkness. *Into the flood again.* I hear the music in my mind and picture my body leaping, completely unencumbered, through the air.

I close my eyes to block out the terror of feeling so alone. Open them to find Nora close by my side. "Hey, Sleepyhead," she croons. "You did need a rest." I hate myself that I feel so pleased to see her. "I have a surprise for you. Can you get up?"

Before this year's state fair, I could not have imagined the physical exertion required to rise from a bed while handcuffed to that same bed.

We manage through the whole transfer of hardware without incident. I notice that Nora has made a major adjustment to our set of handcuffs. She's wrapped them in moleskin, that material that you stick on the back of your shoes to prevent blisters. The soft fabric hugs the metal bracelet of the handcuffs. Just my side, which is, I think, a bit melodramatic of her. I want to tell her to stop being such a martyr. It's not like there's going to be a moment when I'm like, *But Nora, you were so considerate and self-sacrificing in the ways you kept me chained to you.*

She fastens that second set and then unlocks the set connected to the bed. I tug, just a little bit, and grudgingly admit it feels better. "Thank you. That really helps," I force myself to say, trying to keep the bleakness I feel out of my voice.

Nora says, "Oh, you're welcome. But that's not the surprise—I mean, it's related to the surprise, but this isn't it." She stumbles over her words, which I've come to learn means that something matters to Nora. "I was super solution-oriented last night," she announces, and stands nearby patiently as I use the bathroom and brush my teeth. She helps me change into a pair of leggings and fit fresh socks on my feet. We tuck the strands of my greasy hair behind my ears, and then we lumber into the kitchen. I refuse to allow my eyes to roam greedily around the cabin. I refuse to ask Nora about the surprise.

We eat breakfast and I focus on the oatmeal in my bowl. I fuel myself up. I still feel a little woozy.

Nora clears her throat, as if readying for a speech. "We were talking last night about the best ways to dance with our limitations." She raises her wrist just slightly enough that I feel the tiniest pressure. "I worked out an answer. It's maybe a little unconventional. But I think that we'll both see that it helps—you'll have more freedom to move around and I'll be able to dance without worrying about . . . well, I will just know our situation remains secure." Nora coughs again. "Let's go check it out."

Together we shuffle to the far end of the living room. It's hard to coordinate our steps this morning. Nora points to the corner, the one she's already painted and strung lights around. When she shows me, I understand why she needed to stash me in the back room for the night. She needed to move freely without me dangling from her arm. She had to access tools.

She's drilled two bolts on either side of the thick wooden beam that crosses the ceiling of the cabin, then strung a metal cable through those. Looped through the cable is a metal chain with a clip at the end. It's long and sits in a silver pile of links on the floor—it's basically a really long dog leash.

It takes me a moment to soak it in. My eyes move over each element to fully understand the apparatus. I look toward her and she shoots me a shy smile, bashful as if she's preparing herself to fend off my fervent gratitude. Nora plans to hook the metal clip to the handcuff that currently encircles her own wrist to the chain on the floor.

Then I'll be able to run, leap, pirouette, and even sort of spin—up to a point. I think a spin will still risk tangling. Nora breathes in my ear as she leads me to the pile of chain. "I thought I'd hook you up now and just give you a chance to move around, get a sense of the measurements and all. I tried it last night so that I can still help with the choreography. And I also know it's completely secure." She underlines that part with a warning, then continues. "You can explore a little while I clean up after breakfast. Then we can spend some time reviewing the song and working out choreography. My hope is that we can post a finished video by noon. It's still early." Nora says this, but I have no concept of time. My days are now segmented by different lengths of chains. "We didn't post a video yesterday but I'm good with that. I hope you are too. This is going to improve our content so much, Shea. It's a real game changer."

"I see that. Yeah."

"You're really quiet." I know that when Nora says *quiet*, she means *ungrateful*.

"I'm just speechless. I can't believe you did all this. It's so unbelievable, Nora."

"Yeah, well, you know I've been listening to you. I just want the best for us—for our team."

"I know, Nora." And then, because my safety absolutely depends on Nora's mood and level of paranoia: "Thank you so much. It really is extraordinary."

"Of course. It's all for you, Shea." And then I keep my face as placid as possible as Nora hooks me up to my very own dog run.

CHAPTER 21
DELANCEY

We're at lunch when the video posts. My phone buzzes with the notification, along with the phone of pretty much every other person sitting in the cafeteria because I don't know of anyone at Stadium who doesn't follow Shea. If they don't, it's one of those spiritual-rejections-of-online-overexposure . . . and, let's face it, who has time for that?

So around me, 765—minus maybe 12—hands reach for their phones. That's half our school, everyone who has B lunch. The other half sit in study hall, so the proctors are probably losing their minds writing behavior tickets for phone use in class.

We all want to see what Shea posts. We all want to know where she is. The rest of the school believes Shea ran away. They think the content houses in California or Nevada recruited her and she'll post a big reveal in a week or two.

The police came to campus to conduct interviews for two

days. Not two full days. They came twice, set up shop in the counseling office for an hour or two each time, and listened to people Shea and I don't really know claim that she often talked about wanting more exposure, that she'd been acting secretive, that she was really upset about her mom's upcoming marriage.

I hear about this once the cops have packed up and moved on. I hear people comparing theories when I walk through the halls. They whisper behind me as I sit at my desk and wait for class to begin. Sometimes I interrupt them to issue corrections. I say, "You know she could really be in danger, right?" and "When you're just offering guesses then you're sending the police off with false leads." But then I just get defensive dismissals. Worse, they give me pitying looks. No one's intentionally serving up misinformation. I know that. They're just describing the Shea they expect to exist.

At another time, a girl might go missing and the whole school might gather for a moment of silence. Instead, here at B lunch we all bow our heads together and separately watch the reel on our phones. I watch the full 68 seconds and then watch again. There's a second person in the video—a girl our age, but I don't have time for her yet. I see all Shea and only Shea. Lines of text begin cascading down the comment section, and I know that some of the hands typing are right in this room. While I view the video a second time, I feel 765 sets of eyes on me—maybe minus 12, maybe not. It's not impossible to think that everyone is staring at me. They weigh my head down; I can't lift it to meet anyone's scrutiny.

I know why they are staring. Most people think that I only miss Shea's coattails. Some of them assume I'm in love with her. Some of them believe I know exactly where she is.

Next to me, Diana sighs. She feels it too. For a second I feel guilty. The moment I felt my phone vibrate at my hip, I forgot Diana existed. Let alone sat next to me. Now she asks, "You ready to head out?"

"It's gonna feel like a perp walk."

Diana's voice goes loud when she's angry. "Well, it shouldn't feel like that. Let them stare. Shea doesn't look right. You're seeing this too, right, Delancey? These clowns can just keep scrolling. Nobody's gonna do anything to help." Diana starts gesturing wildly at the tables of classmates around us. The low murmur starts and then gains volume. Diana full-on yells over the crowd. "Just go back to your organic corn dogs—nothing to see here."

Diana stomps to the kitchen window and slams her tray down. I sling my bag over my shoulder and keep my eyes down, focused on Shea. Someone jostles me and I almost haul off and hit them. That's how often I function on defense now. But it's only Di, looping her arm through mine. "I'm gathering the troops. We'll set up a situation room, right?"

"Right." I try to sound sure of anything. I'm on my fourth view of the post. Diana texts furiously as we walk. "Jolie is lame and will not leave study hall. What is so hard about asking to go to the restroom? It's like I need to write an instruction manual for these people. We'll use the theater department again?"

"Yeah, I think so. The Black Box." After the second Cure video, we agreed to meet up within a half hour of any post to Shea's channel. We drop anything we need to.

I know that Diana believes me. She doesn't speak the language of sugarcoat. Each time we gather, I half expect the others to quit showing up.

But we get to the room, and they are already sitting at the conference table. Even Jolie. She's crouched by the projector, hooking up her phone to the laptop and her laptop to the projector.

Pearl raps her knuckles on the table. "I think we need to make an agreement right now. We don't read the comments."

"That's right," Di says. "Pearl, that's a good idea. I am telling you, we could all do without that noise. We want to focus on Shea. No comments."

"No comments *now*." I try to keep my voice low, so it doesn't come across like a command. "But there might be information to be found in the comments. Shea might comment, even under a different handle. Whoever has her might comment." I see their looks slide around the room. It scares them when I talk like this, and Shea and I can't lose their allegiance too. "Or whoever she's with. Later we have to read every single comment. And we need to leave our own carefully constructed comments. That's the only way we can reach Shea. Or this other person."

"Or people," Jolie's boyfriend, Marcus, offers.

"People? I only saw one other person, and she seems about

the right age and shape to be attached to that second pair of legs from the last video." Diana slaps the desk.

"That doesn't say anything definitive. It makes more sense that at least two people have her. If we think Shea is being held against her will," Marcus theorizes. "Otherwise, why wouldn't she fight?"

"She could be injured," Jolie says.

"She didn't look injured."

"Well, she sure didn't look good." Diana nods to Jolie. "Projector ready?"

"Yeah. The picture should be clearer this time." Before she hits play, Jolie holds up her hand. "I just want to confirm: We're all just going to cut sixth period. We're okay with that?"

Diana snorts derisively. "You want to tell Shea that we needed to schedule our rescue efforts around Algebra II?"

Marcus says, "Some of us have transcripts to protect, Diana. I'm not saying class is more important, but let's just all make the decision instead of you directing the entire effort the way that—"

"The way that what?" Diana's voice is a blade, slicing through the room. No one fills in the blanks, but we all think it: Marcus meant the way that Shea choreographed our dances. The way that Shea chose songs. The way that she directed everything.

He doesn't know, I remind myself. He just showed up to rehearsals to pick up his girlfriend once in a while and probably thought Jolie should be the one front and center. That's what you're supposed to believe about your girlfriend. It's not Marcus's fault, after all.

"So okay," I say, "let's decide. This is important, right? It's worth skipping class—to me at least. If the academic stakes feel higher for you, we get it." I look around the room and pronounce each word very carefully. "That doesn't mean you don't care about Shea."

"Maybe it means you care a little less about Shea." I shoot Diana a warning look and she holds up her hands. "All right, all right. We all care equally about Shea." She drops her voice to a mutter. "Some of us apparently also really like math."

No one gets up to leave. I'm eager to get started. We've spent enough time on team upkeep. "Okay. Let's start with song choice. Can someone link to the song?"

"It's 'Would?' by Alice in Chains, released in 1992." Jolie keeps typing. "Won a MTV Video Music Award for Best Video from a Film, *Singles*. Also featured in season two of *The Punisher*."

Marcus shrugs. "Well, that's eclectic."

"Oof," Jolie says, grimacing.

"What is it?" She hesitates. "Jolie, come on."

"'Written by Jerry Cantrell in memory of his friend Andy Wood, the deceased lead singer of the band Mother Love Bone,'" she reads.

"Well, I doubt that's relevant," Marcus says firmly.

"Do we know that, though?" Diana asks.

"It's an angle. But wherever she is, I can't see Shea being able to research the origin of each song," I point out. "Grunge really isn't Shea's speed." She hasn't been harboring some secret grief for the guy from Mother Love Bone.

"What about the time period?" Pearl bites the eraser of her pencil, thinking. "It's all late eighties, early nineties, so maybe Shea's with someone older."

"The girl in the video seems our age, maybe even younger. It's not going to be her kind of music either."

"We don't know that." The theories fly around the room.

"Whoever took Shea could have taken the other girl too."

"So that would mean someone in their forties is just collecting teenagers and filming them?"

"Right." No one says anything.

"But you know? Shea does that—she likes bringing back old songs and reintroducing them. She's been all over retro lately," Diana says, and we all nod, reassuring ourselves. No one wants to believe that Shea is held captive by a fifty-year-old Pearl Jam fan.

I say, "I think we need to watch the video frame-by-frame. Let's pull up the song lyrics and zoom in on Shea."

It's harder to see her on the larger image projected on the wall. Somehow, she looks farther away.

"Check out the way Shea looks at the other dancer," Jolie says. "Does anyone else think she's afraid of the girl?" It's true, every now and then Shea looks to her side, like she's checking to make sure the other girl is pleased. Sometimes Shea looks directly at the camera and then right at the girl, like she's aiming to pull the gaze of the audience to the other dancer. It works; I follow her eye movements and concentrate on the face of the other dancer.

The girl looks vaguely familiar. She also looks like Shea, so I chalk it up to the way Shea's fans will glom on to these tiny details of her appearance and sort of claim them for themselves. They both wear heavy eye makeup, full-on masks that cover whole swathes of their faces. Like they're playing Power Rangers or Zorro. It's a look, for sure. Very Ziggy Stardust. Shea's done up in a bright violet color, which alarmed me at first. I worried she chose it to cover bruises, but I don't see a trace of that when we examine the close-ups.

We do notice weirdness with Shea's right arm. Whether it's the camera angle or her movements, the picture goes fuzzy right over her arm, no matter where Shea moves. Jolie, who has as much tech expertise as any of us, pulls up the video on her laptop and nerds out with her zoom button. We still don't land on much of an answer. "See? You can see how it's wavy right there. The other girl's arm doesn't do that. It doesn't happen on Shea's left arm. But if you look at every shot, her right arm blurs in the same place."

We watch again. "She keeps looking down at that spot too," Diana observes. "Hey, turn up the sound—see how the song lines up."

We stand closer to the screen and listen. *So I made a big mistake / Try to see it once my way.* Each time that chorus plays, Shea looks to her left arm. As soon as Pearl points it out, it seems so obvious. I can't unsee it. Shea even stares directly at the camera, widens her eyes, and looks down at her left arm. She's all but pointing.

"How is her arm a mistake?" Marcus asks. "Maybe she injured it? Could she have written a message on her arm?"

"Why would she write a message on her arm of all places?" Di snaps. "Goodness. That doesn't make any sense."

"I'm just thinking aloud. You're so critical."

Pearl moves to stand between Diana and Marcus before they use their own arms to throw punches. I watch her lips move; she repeats the lyrics in time with the video. "Guys, enough," she says, but she's not fully focused on the fight erupting on either side of her. Her lips move—singing, thinking. "Maybe she's just using that phrase to get our attention. It's the next line: *Try to see it once my way*. Right? Do you get it?"

"I don't get it." I hear the defeat in my voice. The heads around me shake too.

"Maybe she knows the video will look a different way." Pearl falters as she speaks, like she's fitting the pieces together. "Yeah. Like see it her way—the real way."

"So that the way we're seeing it—"

"Is not real. You mean it's edited?" Marcus asks.

Jolie nods. "That would account for the blurring. Final Cut does that sometimes. But why just edit her arm?"

"She's wounded. I think she's injured. You can see when she hits fourth and fifth position, her arm drags, like it meets resistance."

"You think she has a cast?" Jolie pauses the video and we stare at Shea. We go back and watch again. The only other time Shea looks directly at the camera is during the chorus. Layne Staley howls about trying to get home. He sings full throttle, his voice raw with pain, and Shea beams her brightest smile at the camera. And then her head jerks. It looks like maybe she shivers.

"Right there! Could she be shaking her head, maybe?" Marcus taps the screen.

"I think that's reaching," Diana says.

"Yeah, well, we're supposed to be reaching. We're freeze-framing a TikTok video for hidden messages to see if our friend was kidnapped."

"You think she's saying she didn't run?" It's what I believe, of course. I've never believed that Shea just ran. But it almost hurts to ask out loud.

"She *could* be saying that," Jolie says gently.

"Does the other girl do any of this stuff? The pointed looks? The twitches?" We watch the video again, this time fully focused on the girl beside Shea. I swear I recognize her, but I can't quite place it. It's like when you wake up and remember sort of what the dream was about. "Does anyone know her? I feel like we know her?"

"From the fair?" Marcus asks. "Does anyone remember seeing her at the fair?"

"The makeup makes it hard."

"I know her from somewhere," I tell them. "Maybe from the meet and greet? That would make sense." I try to picture the wooden amphitheater, the way Shea kept smiling and signing.

I think I spent the entire time pouting, resentful that her mom had booked an appearance on our night out. I was so focused on feeling slighted. I wasn't paying close enough attention. This girl could have been there. I wouldn't have noticed.

Marcus barks out, "Hey—hold up there. It's another blurry spot. See? By the other girl's foot?"

"Another cast?" Diana asks like even she thinks the suggestion is nonsense.

"It's not fuzzy *on* the other girl's foot. It goes fuzzy *near* her foot. Like on the floor. You can barely see it because of the grain on the floor but it does blur." Jolie stands up and traces a line from the floor directly to Shea's right arm. "Do you see it? It's like a line or—"

"A chain." Diana is the only one bold enough to say it out loud. I know she's right because all the air seems to leave the room at once. We all just stand there, staring at the screen and trying to breathe. When you know it, it's easy enough to imagine it—the straight line running across the floor and up to Shea's arm, the way it weighs down her movements. She keeps directing our eyes to her wrist, insisting we notice. They way her jumps pull back just a little and her smile doesn't reach her eyes.

"It's not just the lyrics. It's the band name." I choke saying it. "Alice in Chains."

CHAPTER 22
NORA'S PHONE

Holy crap—Shea, you're a legend. Insane. Love this song. Love this surprise.

Worth waiting for. Wow. Picking up the pieces of my jaw off the floor.

More of this please.

Going to go digging through my dad's record collection now.

Folks, this is how Seattle does it. PNW born and raised.

Forget Seattle. This is T-Town all the way. Jerry Cantrell's song. Shea Davison's moves.

Listen leave room for all the brilliance. All love here, Shea.

You worried us, girl. Shea you seem back on track. But what's with the body double?

These videos remind me of those exercise videos where the

slow, unfit girl does her own set of moves in the back. Tell your friend to get her own channel.

Hot song, Shea, but you still look rough. What's going on? Can someone say dead eyes? And what's up with your hair?

Why do you only feature male singers? What happened to sisterhood?

Shea, I'm signing back up for ballet. This is ferocious.

Shea, honey, the dancing is incredible but we all miss you. No intro? No diary? What? Don't you still love us?

Does anyone else get the feeling that other girl is holding Shea hostage?

Not laughing—alarmed. Shea looks ragged and dirty. Reporting. Shea, seriously, get yourself together. You're scaring us.

Maybe the other girl isn't supposed to be dancing?

Anyone notice some crazy editing? Or did my screen go weird?

What's up with the edits? That's not like you, Shea. What's up?

Can't you just edit the other girl out?

Can we get #othergirl trending?

Does anyone else get Katy Perry Left Shark vibes from that other girl?

Hey. It's been more than a week without contact, Nora. Unacceptable. You're lucky I talked Sonny out of calling the *police and reporting that truck stolen. Get it together. You're out of control.*

Shea, we just need to know you're safe. That's all you need to do is text back the word Safe.

Honestly, Nora, I love you, but I don't know how we move forward from this. You need to call me.

Message received. We're coming for you, Alice. Stay strong.

CHAPTER 23
NORA

We need only four takes to record the video. Part of that is Shea—she's just that talented. She coils up her muscles. She unleashes. She explodes.

This time it was the combination of Shea and the song selection. Maybe the effects we chose together—the sparse lighting, the dark tones. I'll take a little credit for those contributions. But the song did most of the work for us—unexpected and mighty. I've never thought of rage as gorgeous before. But Shea and I showed that. We astounded people.

And I found a way for Shea to dance the way Shea needs to dance—the way a storm rolls in and splits open the sky. Shea could not have done that safely, had I not spent most of the night rigging up the living room system. Drilling holes and testing out different kinds of clasps and catches. And then I spent hours at the kitchen table editing out every silver link of chain, every glint of metal around her wrist. So me taking on a little bit of credit for this video feels warranted. Shea would not have created something so remarkable in her bedroom back in Tacoma. I know that. Deep down, she must know that too.

When my phone starts chiming, Shea's eyes flicker to mine. We know we've done amazing work.

"Do you have my channel loaded on your phone now?" She doesn't accuse me; she just asks.

"Yes." I answer just as simply. And then I correct her. "*Our* channel." The phone dings again. It feels incredible to think that right this minute, people are devouring this thing I created. My phone practically pulses in my hands. Reactions flood in from all over. I can't get over it. I never could have imagined it. I feel generous. I ask her, "Do you want to read some of the comments together?"

"It's not always the best thing, Nora." Shea has the audacity to look worried. We just recorded the best video to ever launch from her channel and she can't bring herself to admit that. "Especially if it's something you believe really turned out amazing. You know I believe that too. It's an awesome video. But sometimes it's better to take some time and just enjoy that feeling of success on your own. Really just relish it. Because other people are just going to tear it down. Not everyone." She rushes to correct herself. "But some people—that's all they do. It's pretty much why they watch." She sighs. "Nora, I just want you to have the chance to enjoy this feeling of success. We created something really cool today."

"Oh, did we?" Could she be any more condescending? "When was the last time one of your solo videos racked up so many views so quickly? I mean, I've been there for all of it and certainly boosted your signal, but I don't recall anything like this. Maybe early on, but that was back when the platform itself was simpler. Think of all that we're competing with now."

"I didn't mean—"

"Well, then what *did* you mean, Shea? And who's tearing you down anyway? Do you know how many hours I've spent trying to think of the perfect comment—something witty and memorable? That stood out among all the other lines of adoration. Just so that maybe once you would notice? It would have set off fireworks in my heart if you even hit like. I tried so hard. For what? So you could whine about a few critics."

"I do feel lucky. I appreciate my followers, Nora."

"*Our* followers, Shea."

"Of course. Yes. I don't mean to imply that you're not ready for feedback. Maybe it's just that I wasn't. It hurt me; that's all. I don't want that for you. I don't like to look at reactions right away. I try to go for a walk or out with my friends."

"That's really wholesome of you, Shea." The phone vibrates again—three notifications in quick succession.

"But I'm excited too. This is a whole new world, after all. It's our channel now. Maybe it's time to handle it differently. I'd be honored if we could sit together and see some of the responses."

"Really?" Not for the first time, I remind myself that Shea Davison is a stellar performer.

"Of course, really. I'm so sorry, Nora. I didn't mean to discourage you. I just get anxious. It's like post–stage fright. That's my issue, though."

"Will you be okay? We don't need to make a big deal of it if it's going to cause a panic attack or something. We're not close enough for any kind of medical help—we've talked about that before."

"I know. I'll be fine. It helps to experience this as a team. I hadn't expected that."

Again, I watch her carefully. She seems earnest enough.

"Well, you've done group dances before. I've seen them."

"I know, but it was still all me, you know? This feels like the two of us creating something together." Shea Davison actually says that to me. She looks directly at me and speaks straight from her heart.

"Well, okay then. Let's do it. We'll sit right here." I pat the spot next to me on the sofa. And that's something else. She can walk over basically by herself and sit. It feels a ton more normal. Except for the clanking when the chain drags on the floor.

Shea hears it too. "Sorry." I don't comment. I don't like to talk about the handcuffs. Every time they flash, they remind me that Shea would not have chosen to join me at the cabin. I had to go to extraordinary lengths to get her here. She didn't have the kind of faith I did in our eventual partnership. But that's okay, I remind myself. We're here now.

"How do you usually read them?" I ask her. "First or most recent?"

"First," Shea answers immediately. "It lets me follow along if people interact with each other."

I hold the phone between us. It moves a little and I realize that my hand trembles.

"Are you nervous?" she asks kindly.

"I didn't think so."

"It could also be adrenaline. You're all pumped up from the energy you're generating."

"Okay. I'm ready now." I refresh the phone. The first comment seems fine enough. I look to Shea and she smiles and nods. I keep scrolling. Again, more about Shea. That's to be expected, though. We don't even introduce me by name. We can't yet because of certain circumstances.

There's a lot of talk about the music choice, and I feel at least partially responsible for that stroke of brilliance. Tons of comments compare our video favorably to the Shea Davison standards of the olden days.

So I'm still feeling pretty good—lots of positivity. Shea's followers get it—they really seem to understand what we're aiming for. They're still just Shea followers. It's still all Shea. It makes me realize we should have introduced me more deliberately. Even if I chose a stage name or something. But okay. Now I know. That has to take priority for the next video.

I hear Shea suck in her breath before I read the first really mean comment in its entirety. I make myself reread it so that I know exactly how they worded it. I tell myself that's just one person. One voice in a chorus of praise really. But then someone else responds to the first commenter. And then someone else. They start riffing on "the other girl." Everyone seems to have a joke at my expense.

Shea sets her hand on my arm, ever so gently. "Nora, I'm so sorry. Maybe we should stop for now. Especially when a video trends, it starts a frenzy. Folks forget we're real people. They're just commenting quickly. They're not thinking." She just yammers on and on, as if she's not secretly pleased to keep reigning as queen ballerina of TikTok.

"Could you please just shut your perfect, famous mouth?" Her lips snap closed, and at least that vaguely satisfies me. "I just want to be alone now, please."

"You should really turn off the phone, even just for tonight. We'll do something else. We'll step back, get to know each other more."

"Please just go."

"Okay, I get it. Nora, I do understand. I'm here if you need me."

I laugh—a harsh, jagged sound that scrapes through the cabin. "Well, Shea, where else would you be?"

She takes a few steps toward the back bedroom, and at first, I don't notice the issue. My head faces down, soaking in the online observations of people who apparently despise me. I hear the metal clank as Shea stops moving. It's wicked to smirk at her while I storm past her and head to the back bedroom myself. But it helps. I slam the door shut behind me and picture Shea standing forlornly in the middle of the front room, unable to reach the bedroom because she's firmly tethered to the wall.

In the privacy of the little room, I keep reading. Each line slices and stings. They think of me as Shea's clumsy shadow—*the other girl*. I'm the worst feature of a Shea Davison video, a weird exception that ruins something otherwise extraordinary. And I can't just dismiss them because they also love the same pieces I love—the unusual song choice, the contrast between the music's barely reined chaos and our deliberate choreography. They notice all those aspects; they just attribute them fully to Shea. Me? I don't count for anything. I just take up space.

Line by line, I start responding before thinking it through. At first, I argue in my head, the way you do when someone's attacking you and you know their accusations are irrational and unfair. You think through your arguments. And then you land on an excellent point, one you feel compelled to share.

I keep it general at first, the way Shea might. Although I've never seen her post a response. Sometimes Shea hits the like button and in rare moments answers with a red heart emoji.

I start by thanking people who posted kind comments. I try to establish that we create as partners now. So I write *Thanks! We worked really hard on that!* Or *Thank you for noticing—we love that part of the song too.* I try to build bridges with the folks who notice the Washington connection. *Neither of us can claim Seattle roots but we both love Washington!* That keeps it vague enough. I'm smart about it. I don't release any details about myself.

My comments sound like the way Shea talks. Any true follower would recognize that. I emulate her relentless cheerfulness. When I think a response is ready to post, I add one more kind word, one more exclamation point. I stay on-brand.

I don't intend to give airtime to cruel comments. But then people start responding to my responses. In real time. An actual conversation. *Is this the royal we, Shea?* Someone else asks *What's going on with all the plurals?* And then suddenly it feels like someone must be staring straight into the cabin windows. Because someone writes *Hold up, Sheatown . . . I bet we have Other Girl on the line now.*

Other Girl, give us a name. Where'd you learn to dance like a wounded owl? Is this some kind of charity campaign where Shea makes Other Girl's Dream come true? I can't keep up. I freeze. And then Devo comments *Who said Other Girl is keeping Shea hostage? Best explanation for this trainwreck.*

Then I have to dive in: *LOL You're all hilarious. Way to haze the newbie. I recognize most of your handles. Longtime follower turned collaborator here. Shea and I are so excited for the next run of videos. More on the way!* I hit send, feeling confident. I'm rising above, but standing up for myself, reminding folks that Shea and I are real people just like them.

They circle like turkey vultures. They dive and peck. *Is*

this Shea's mom? Is this like a bachelorette party thing? Put down
Shea's phone, Shea's mom.

IKR? Who says LOL?

I think it stands for Listen, Othergirl Lies.

Yas! Devo. Love that.

I hear whistling in my ears. My eyes sting at the corners. I scroll
down, hoping for any tiny positive comment. Toward me and not
Shea—someone who might understand a sliver of how hard I've
worked. Maybe I haven't had the private lessons or the hours of
rehearsal time. I've made do. Nobody gives me free hours at a
studio. I don't travel through the world with an entourage.

I read every comment, even the vile ones, hoping someone
has seen me. And that's when I read it. The rest of the words
fall off the page. *Message received. We're coming for you.* And they
call her Alice.

The whistling in my ears ramps up to sirens. I sat out there
at the kitchen table. She watched me. Zooming and clicking and
making the tiniest of adjustments. I erased any trace of the cut
on Shea's arm or the restraints, which we sadly need for her own
safety. The whole time she watched me work, Shea hoped for my
failure. *Alice in Chains.* She chose the music for the message—
not the lyrics but the band name.

I drop the phone on the bed and stand up, head to the door,
and then stop. The feelings streaming through me scare me. I
want to yank Shea to the floor. I want to hit her and hear the
bones in her face crunch.

A thick pottery mug sits on the bedside table. The replacement for the one she broke. There's still amber liquid puddled at the bottom. I've taken care of Shea in every way possible. I gave her space and time and rest and care. 6,548 people have already shared this morning's video. And that number is climbing. 22,000 likes. I was building brilliance while Shea was encrypting messages.

The mug has a formidable heft to it. I can't explain why but I want to slam it over and over against my own eye socket. I want something to hurt in a way I can expect. No more surprises. I hold the mug as far from my face as possible and then whip it toward my right cheek. But I balk. I jerk my hand away at the last second. I hurl it toward the window. It's heavy in my hand and it feels like such a relief to let go. Everything shatters at once—the mug, the window. Glass and ceramic shards rain down on the sill. A jagged hole in the window lets in the cold wind.

Let them come. They'll still need to find us. And Shea won't have the opportunity to disappoint me again.

CHAPTER 24
SHEA

At first, when I hear glass shatter, a surge of hope washes over me. I see it play out the way it does in action movies. The S.W.A.T. team swoops in. An officer dangles from a helicopter line and then kicks in a window. Rescue accomplished.

I only hear Nora's voice, though. No one yells for her to get on the floor. No one demands to know where I am.

Behind the knotty pine door of the cabin's back bedroom, Nora rants. Her voice pitches up and down as if she's arguing with someone. At first, I think maybe she's on the phone. Maybe she has finally called Helen. Helen will urge her to go on home, to drop me off at the feed store in whatever hick town Nora hauled me past. Helen will threaten to send in the cavalry. Helen will plead with Nora, who will eventually break down and agree. I am certain that Nora is back there yelling into the phone, putting up one last stand against Helen's good and steady sense. I scurry as close to the door as the stupid chain will allow, trying to listen to plans come together for our imminent departure.

I can't hear her words clearly, just the rise and fall of her tone and volume. Sudden shouting and the occasional cackle. It's the cackle that first gets me. The sick feeling starts roiling in my stomach. Nora never pauses to listen; no one interrupts her. If she's on the phone, I don't think there's a person on the other side of the line.

The more I eavesdrop, the more I am certain: It's not a conversation that I'm listening to at all. It's just Nora back there, destroying herself with online comments. As soon as she suggested tracking reactions, I knew this would happen. TikTok is not kind; comment sections are not welcoming places. Nora was excited, and she had reason to be. We made a really kickass video. I mean, it's not worth being kidnapped for or anything. But the Alice in Chains video will go viral. I know it.

And if our video goes viral, there will be backlash. That's the cycle. People will seize on the one weak piece—the part that doesn't quite fit or keep the beat. They will tear that weak piece down, especially if she's a hesitant and basic-looking girl.

I knew my followers would decimate Nora. I counted on it. But now they've pushed Nora off the narrow edge she'd balanced on. She's back there, breaking glass and ranting at commenters as if they're right there in the bedroom with her. I've set something in motion now that I don't know how to rein in.

My own cell phone, with its mint-green case, sits on the top shelf near the kitchen. Even if I drag myself back closer and elongate my body in my deepest stretch, I won't be able to reach it.

But I can't just sit here and wait while Nora deteriorates. Maybe she's hurt herself. Maybe she's tired. This could be the weakest she will be.

"Nora," I call out. "Please. I need to use the bathroom." I try to sound as pitiful as possible. She doesn't answer. She's still ranting and raging. "Nora, please. I've to go!" I full-on bellow—like a real put-the-lotion-in-the-basket moment. "Nora, I just need to use the bathroom and I can't reach. Please, Nora."

"Stop it. Shut up. I can't think." The door muffles her voice, but I hear her just fine. Nora sounds stressed. She sounds like someone who may not be thinking so carefully. Who might be distracted. Who could be overcome.

"I can't think either. I have to go so badly. Please, I don't want to pee on the floor. You have to treat me like a human being. Please just let me go to the bathroom, Nora."

"Enough, okay. I hear you. You're so needy, Shea. You're spoiled. Self-centered. I don't know how you've managed to trick hundreds of thousands of people into believing you're worth their time and energy."

"I'm so sorry, Nora." She comes out of the room and looks different—wild-eyed and disheveled. Her eyes don't focus on me. She's still talking much too loudly. I fight my instinct to try to calm her down. I've been placating Nora for more than eight days. It's only gotten me a longer chain. "Were those comments harsh?

I hope my followers didn't attack your dancing. I'm sorry—what am I saying? I mean *our* followers. Did our followers attack your dancing, Nora?"

"Shut up. You know very well that they did. Do you have to use the bathroom or not?" She holds the tiny silver key to the cuffs between her thumb and her index finger. Usually, she wears the key on a chain around her neck. There's one key for both sets of cuffs. I watch her pull the chain over her head.

"I do." I make my voice sound strangled, like I can barely speak. I nod vigorously and shove my wrist into her face. She snaps the second set of cuffs on me. But not on her. The one set just dangles from my wrist.

If we were climbing, the equivalent would be unhooking the first carabiner without fastening the second. Suddenly, I hang there, suspended between confinement and freedom. I don't dare look down. I can't cause Nora's eyes to follow mine and see that she's forgotten to snap the other side around her own wrist.

"Thanks, Nora. You're the best. Why don't I say that? To our followers? Why don't you let me sign in? I can even record a video. I can tell them how much work you did on all the best parts of the 'Would?' video. How you discovered the song and coached me through the choreography. Right? Let me log on and tell our followers it was all you."

She fits the tiny key in the lock and turns. Right as the hinge opens, Nora zeroes in her gaze at me. "Really? Because from what I remember, you chose the band. Alice in Chains." She smirks. She blinks. She shakes the set of handcuffs. Right at that moment, I realize that Nora knows why. Someone online understood my message. Someone's coming to help. At that same moment, Nora realizes she never hooked herself to the second set of handcuffs. We stand there, facing each other, in the center of the cabin. For the first time in days, I am unbound.

Panic hits Nora's eyes. I'm sure she sees it reflected in mine. For a long moment, we both freeze.

Then I run.

I sprint straight toward the front door of the cabin. It's not a big house; it can't take me more than five long strides, but it feels like forever. Nora screams my name behind me, and my hand reaches to slide the deadbolt while I'm still springing forward. I fling the bolt to the side and yank the door open.

My hand braces against the inside of the doorframe to try to pull my body forward faster—away from Nora, who charges behind me. There's no screen door. Outside, it's that time just before the sun starts to set. The tall trees filter out most of the light. I step through. My right foot crosses over onto the woven doormat. It slips a little and I slide but manage to steady myself.

I have no plan, just a direction—out. Forward. Behind me, Nora shrieks, but I don't turn. All I see is the outside, the open land around the small house where she has kept me. My body is mostly out. I use my hand on the door to propel myself forward.

That's when the door slams. It thunders closed. It doesn't snap shut. It cracks against my arm and brings me to my knees.

I can't see the trees outside. Just the woven welcome mat below my feet and the dusty bricks of the front walkway.

I taste vomit in my mouth. I smell pine and the iron scent of old blood. I make myself open my eyes and look at my arm.

It dangles. The angle of how my arm hangs is all wrong. Thin threads of blood seep from my old wound, but the whole limb looks less like an arm anymore. Next to me, I feel the old door quiver. But of course, it's not as if the door slammed itself.

Beside the door, Nora stands panting. "What have you done, Shea?" Her voices sound weary and disgusted. She crouches down and wraps one arm around my waist. She drags me up. My arm flops and hot, blank pain shoots all the way to my shoulder. I don't recognize the sounds coming from me as my own voice. They're moans. They're the chorus to an old song about broken people surrendering. Nora's got her breath back. She hisses in my ear as she locks the handcuff back in place. "Why I am not surprised? No one can trust you. You do your absolute best to ruin everything, don't you?"

CHAPTER 25

NORA

I don't recognize the sounds coming from Shea as human. I make a fair attempt to move her gently, but she's heavy and uncooperative. She's not crying or screaming. She sounds like a balloon deflating. I tell her, "I don't know what you were thinking. I explained to you how isolated we are out here. I can't drive you to a hospital. We won't see a doctor for a while."

I deposit Shea on the bed and get to work securing her. She whines and whimpers.

"Do you want to talk to your followers now, Shea?" I offer. "Maybe you want to make a video now? Maybe there's another band you wish to highlight?"

I sigh. "You think I'm so very terrible. You're better off running into the wilderness. I should have let you go. Let night fall and the temperature drop—you would have frozen in those woods." I hear myself. And hate myself. I feel this anger, this icy fist closing in my throat. I can't swallow past it without tears springing into the corners of my eyes. Who are we anyway? I could look in the mirror right now. All I would see is unfamiliar spite.

Everything seemed like it was becoming real, and now I feel it slipping away from me. Shea's hurt and I cannot seem to put my rage aside to fix it. I can't step around it in order to try to make things right.

Each time I try to clasp the mechanism around Shea's wrist, she pulls her arm away. Then she moans all over again because of the movement. She's incredibly stubborn. I'm trying to help her.

"Stop it." I try to keep my voice calm. "I'm handling your arm really carefully, so that you don't hurt yourself even more. We're going to connect your left arm to the bed this time. So that we don't aggravate your injury. Because I'm a responsible person. I'm not a cruel person."

I remind her, "You have no idea where we are. You're delirious. I'm responsible for your safety. You know what? We're going to use both sets of cuffs. How's that?"

Shea just shakes her head at me. I move firmly and carefully. I fasten the one set of cuffs to the bedframe. Then I use the second on her wrists. Her shoulders shake, like she's crying, but knowing Shea, it's just another performance meant to manipulate me.

"What video should we record now, Shea?" She buries her face in her arms. "You don't seem to have any quick comebacks now. Do me a favor and stay right there, okay?" I cross to the tiny linen closet and rummage around on the bottom shelf—the one with all the cleaning supplies. I bring out an old metal bucket and leave it next to the bed. "Do you still need to pee, Shea? It seemed like a real desperate need before. Let me solve that for you—here's your bucket again. You have bathroom access all the time. No need to wait for me to take a break from being verbally abused by your followers!"

My rage is a train that has exited the station. I can't put on the brakes or hold it back. Shea sits huddled in the top half of the bed. The more she sobs, the angrier I get. She betrayed me, after all. I had to read all those terrible things about myself. As usual, everyone adores her. No one ever notices the ugly side of Shea. Unless I show them. I grab my phone and start taking photos. "Maybe let's get some pics for a follow-up post? That should rack up the likes, right, Shea? Come on, it's so important to you that people know every detail of your life. Give the people what they want."

"Stop it, stop it, Nora, please!" she howls. I feel very little. Maybe I feel somewhat bored. The more Shea breaks down, the more composed I feel.

"Okay, we obviously could use a bit of space. I'm going to head out for a little bit, clear my head." Shea whips up her head in alarm. "Careful, there. That looks like it hurt." I sail into the kitchen, grab my keys, and come back to shake them at her. They make a cheerful jingling sound.

"Nora! Nora!" For someone I once considered so independent, Shea whines like a child.

"What?" The word slashes through the air. It could draw blood. There's nothing Shea can say that will erase the comments I just read, the hate I had to absorb. "I'm taking the truck," I tell her. "Don't wait up."

My bravery evaporates as soon as I close the front door behind me. A few days have passed since I last drove; my skills may have rusted. And of course, each day that's passed has increased the chance that Sonny has reported his truck stolen. I try not to let that fact faze me. I'll drive carefully, I tell myself. I have errands to run.

Sitting in the cab, gathering my courage, I catch sight of the silver generator by the cabin's back door. Its heavy black cord snakes power to the house. It turns out, I'm not finished processing my anger. I hop down from the truck and yank the cord loose. I hope it gets real cold when I'm gone. Shea will lie there feeling sorry for herself. Maybe, as the chill and the dark set in, she'll gradually understand her situation could get even worse.

I climb back in the truck, turn the key in the ignition, and remind myself to drive steady on these empty roads. No one's out here looking to pull me over. While the engine warms, I plug in my phone and resist the urge to open any app besides the navigation. I see notifications piling up but I'm not like Shea—I have a little bit of dignity. I can go on with my day without obsessing over the likes and shares.

Besides, I want to keep my driving to daylight. The closest shopping mall is a good eighty miles away. The roads up here are narrow and empty. I drive a while before I see another driveway, even longer before I pass a house facing right up to the road. I'm not so worried about home security cameras, people don't keep those up here . . . and if they do, they're not checking every pickup that travels past.

I avoid bridges because of cameras. When I hit main roads, I stay to the middle lane. My chest constricts as the mile markers tick down. When I drive by a state trooper's car parked in a lot, I grip the truck's wheel, grit through the instinct to veer. I keep my eyes straight on the road. I keep going.

At the mall, I move with similar purpose. I don't know what I thought would happen—emerging in the world with my own videos gathering momentum on TikTok. I know, logically, I won't get recognized, but I still wear a hoodie tight around my face, keep my gaze down, and avoid mall security.

It takes me a while to find exactly what I need: the hardware store, the card shop, the pharmacy. I keep my stops short and don't browse. I take careful account of my spending although I expect that before our money runs out, someone will head up to the cabin to bring us home.

I try not to spend too much time thinking about how this all ends. Every now and then, I make sure to send Helen a vague text. *Try not to worry. I'll turn back soon.* Just yesterday I sent, *When I need you, could you meet me back at Sonny's place? Don't want to show up on my own.* She probably knows it's a stall tactic, but most likely Helen needs that time too. She has her own family now; she can't keep driving up from California to help Sonny and me hate each other a little less. Eventually, though, someone's going to pull up in the drive. A hand will go on and bang on the door. Or else Sonny will just push on through, yelling and tracking in dirt.

I could double back, pack Shea into the car and drop her off at a hospital on the way. How much time would it take for someone to sort through her story? I could get back to Tacoma and lie low. I already know I won't go through with it, but I like picturing the quiet, orderly days I could craft. I could live a small life parallel to Shea's grand one. Every once in a while, I could catch a glimpse of her.

No matter what happens, Shea will return to much fanfare—at home, at school, online. Every aspect of her life will expand. She doesn't realize yet that I've given her that. Even if she understood, she's unlikely to appreciate it.

The bags slam against my shins as I rush from store to store. That panic sets in—is she okay? Is she comfortable? Today's lesson is important—I know that. Folks just cannot walk all over me, taking advantage and persecuting me. Each time I catch myself worrying, I check my notifications. And then the hurtful words stoke my anger all over again.

At the craft store, there's a moment when I wonder if the girl behind the counter recognizes me. I'm buying crystals. I know they're pricey but the checkout girl at Michael's doesn't need to know how carefully I've already weighed the cost. It bothers me when she goes so slow, like she's half waiting for me to change my mind.

"Is there a problem?" I inquire.

"Course not," she says, but then she asks, "What are you making? You know, we have alternative brands too. The Crystal Radiance is just so pricey. The off-brands catch the light just as well."

"I'm good, thanks." I pull a wad of creased bills out of the zippered pocket of my jacket.

"You're sure?"

"Do you know how many people are going to see these crystals catch the light?" At first, she doesn't respond. "Seriously," I say, "do you?" She shakes her head. She looks past me apologetically to the woman behind me, who's carrying an armful of fake feathers and shifting her weight from side to side as if they are heavy.

"*Nine hundred thousand* people will see these crystals. Probably more than that now." I whip out my phone to check the rising number of followers. "Correction: Nine-hundred eighty-eight thousand. So I feel comfortable splurging for the extra sparkle."

"Yeah, all right," the girl says with a shrug in her voice, but I catch her watching me more closely, trying to place me. It's just a tiny sliver of a moment, but I understand a little more of Shea's entitlement. Why shouldn't we insist on receiving a little respect? There's a reason people call us influencers.

But of course, I'm not Shea—every interaction with another human being makes me nervous. Every glance my way has me ducking. I remember I'd vowed to move about the mall inconspicuously. Yet here I am blowing cover at the craft store because someone questioned my taste in Swarovski knockoffs. I don't toss my hair and glare over my shoulder on my way out the way I bet Shea would. I lower my head and skitter away like a roach.

It doesn't matter. It dumbfounds me to rely on the same refrain I've leaned on for years. Through my mom's illness, through the quiet of her death. Through Sonny's building anger, and Helen's leaving, I leaned on those same three words: *It doesn't matter.* 988,000 followers. Closing in on one million. Things are supposed to matter now.

But I have the real treasure stashed back at the cabin, mail ordered months ago and packed along with all the rest of our necessary supplies. Just this morning I figured out how to best present my gift. After today's revelation, I've decided on some adjustments. It doesn't matter what the staff at the craft store in Cowlitz County think of me.

Shea and I have added so many followers in less than twenty-four hours. I marvel all the way through the mall, scrolling through the list of newly added names. I pronounce some of them aloud as I walk—dozens of people who know who I am. Or at least they know Shea. Soon enough, they'll know me too.

Of course it's a mistake, but I can't help peeking at the comments. I'm still the hot topic of mockery. Othergirl is still trending. There's a whole comment thread of memes: my photo beside some other famously bad dancers—the lady from *Seinfeld*, the Super Bowl Shark, a can of cranberry sauce emptied into a bowl.

I try. I straighten my shoulders and steel my spine and dare the shoppers around me to notice me. I step confidently. No one recognizes me. No one flutters near me, scrolling quickly on their phone to confirm my value. I don't make the kind of ripple in the world that Shea does.

But Shea isn't here. And I'm the only one who knows where to find her. There's power in that. I grip my keys in my hand, shake them gently so that they clink. I have more options than I've ever had before.

In the parking lot, a woman slows down walking by me. Loading up packages in the row of seats behind the cab, I feel her before I see her. I work to keep my calm before turning around. Does she know me or Sonny? Does she recognize my apparently lame dancing?

She's not in our target demographic. She looks older and wears one of those sweatshirts with a built-in collar. It's got cardinals on it—red birds settled on a wooden fence. I study the birds on her shirt while I work up the nerve to look up to her face.

I almost sigh out loud with relief. I don't know her. She calls me "Honey"—not my name. "Honey," she says, "are you here on your own?"

"Ma'am?" I don't understand why she's speaking to me. I look past her. There's another older woman a few steps away, carefully negotiating the curb's step up.

The lady's friend sees her stopped and backtracks. "Trina?"

But Trina's busy, asking me, "Is your mama here?"

It amazes how much it still hurts to be asked. When I say no, I sound angry. I grip my keys until they dig into the palm of my hand.

"Trina, leave the girl alone. She's just out for some shopping."

The woman in the bird shirt looks at me like she knows all my secrets. "You're so young. How old are you, dear?"

"For goodness' sake, Trina." The friend steps back toward us. "I'm so sorry." She grabs her friend's hand. "Everyone looks young to us." She moves to lead Trina away.

"How's a girl that young here by herself? Where are her friends? Her folks?"

I slam the back door shut and climb up into the driver's seat before Trina convinces her friend to look back at me. The engine turns quick and I back out so fast the women have to jump to clear the path.

My tires squeal and the cab shakes as I careen out of the lot. I pull up to the intersection and turn too quickly onto the highway. I almost get sideswiped by a car speeding by in the middle lane. Horns on either side of me blare.

I pound the steering wheel, try to gather myself back together. I count my breaths in and count my breaths out. If Shea hadn't acted with such a profound lack of gratitude, I wouldn't have been at the mall on my own. We could have wandered around the mall with our heads craned toward each other, giggling and whispering, while people tried to remember where they knew us from. *It doesn't matter*, I remind myself. I ease my foot off the gas, get my speed back under control.

I count the ways I am lucky: the truck has half a tank of gas, enough to get back. I barely missed hitting those women and causing an accident later. I found everything we needed and we still have money to spare.

I can't afford to think about what could have happened if I'd wrecked the truck, or those ladies had attracted the attention of mall security. My fingers fly to my throat, where the small key for our cabin security system rests. I just need to get back home.

The phone chimes one way for upcoming turns and another for TikTok notifications. I can't turn the sound off for one app and not the navigation so I have to listen while Shea's followers pile on. It's hard not to wonder what they're saying about me.

Shea's back there hungry and probably headed toward a deeper understanding of my perspective. Maybe she's willing to acknowledge the sacrifices I've made for her and for the site. We have some items to discuss. Crossing through Packwood, I pass a gas station. I even brake on the empty road and consider. I know inside there's a case with sandwiches, a machine rotating oily hot dogs and Hot Pockets. I had planned to stop for food to bring back. But as I consider the options, my phone goes off again. I remember the names they're calling me all over again. Othergirl decides to keep driving.

Our next video will stun them. That's the promise I hold close to me as I make my way home down the long, empty roads of Western Washington. The deeper the truck treks into the woods, the darker it is outside.

When I finally get home, the look of the cabin startles me. It strikes me as sad. Maybe because I pulled the generator, so it sits dark. Maybe because now it's become a place where Shea would injure herself to escape.

I keep the truck lights on and shine them right at the generator. It still takes me more than a few minutes to hook it back up and get it humming. But I do because I'm ready and capable and all those folks slamming me for daring to dance beside someone with extensive formal training should consider that. They are lucky I'm taking such good care of Shea.

It's hard to balance all the packages in my arms. Of course, there's no one to help me. When I planned out our days, I'd counted on Shea coming around by now. Becoming more cooperative. I had expected eventually she would be able to contribute. *It doesn't matter.* I grab the bags, the boxes, juggle my keys in my hands. I can manage all of it.

The first things I notice are the cold and the quiet. Even stepping inside, I see my breath puff in the freezing air. I set the craft supplies on the table. Shea doesn't call out. I don't hear crying or the squeak of her shifting in the bed.

For a second, I stand in front of her closed bedroom door. Only days ago, I stood in this very spot and panicked, worried something had happened. Worried she had choked or hyperventilated or harmed herself in some other melodramatic way. I know she's fine. We're that in tune with each other now. I don't need to open the door to be sure she's leaning back, wary eyes on the other side of it, waiting for me.

I don't open it. "Shea—"

"I'm—" She interrupts me. She should not interrupt me.

"No, you need to listen right now. Answer my questions without any additional commentary." I sound like Sonny, talking to the man who came to our property for the census. "Do you understand that?"

A silence stretches. Then a sniffle. Finally, Shea responds, "Yes."

"You must be starving." More quiet. "Are you hungry?"

A shorter stretch and then, "Yes."

"Wait a few minutes. I'll be back. That's all, though. I have some projects to finish. I'll need to concentrate, without distractions. I don't want to talk to you."

"But, Nora—"

"Do you understand me?" I pronounce my words very carefully. I will not allow Shea to manipulate me any longer.

"Yes."

"Good. The heat is back on. It should warm up soon. How is your arm? Do you need something for the pain?"

It takes her longer to answer. That probably means yes, she is in pain, but no, she doesn't want medicine. She wants her wits about her.

She's still planning something.

Medicine it is. I take one of my mom's old prescription bottles from the kitchen sill and grind two pills with the rolling pin. That's a lot maybe, but I count on losing some to dust on the wooden pin's surface. I spread a slice of wheat bread with peanut butter and sprinkle the ground powder over the center of the sandwich. I drop the grape jelly directly over the white powder, so its sweetness helps to mask the taste. I doubt it matters. She's hungry enough.

I tear a piece of foil and wrap up the sandwich. I grab an empty bottle of water and fill it at the tap, then tighten the cap. Returning to the bedroom door, I lift my hand to knock and then reconsider. It's not like I need to give anyone privacy.

"I'm coming in, but not to talk." I open the door and switch on the light. Shea ducks down to shield her eyes. I hear the clank of metal tangling with metal.

I keep my face blank. I look at Shea the way I'm used to Sonny looking at me. Impassive. I kneel and roll the water bottle toward her. It goes slowly. We both watch it run up against the foot of the iron bed. Then I skim the wrapped sandwich across the floor too. She grabs at it.

"We can try to figure out a shower in the morning."

I see her open her mouth to thank me and then remember my instructions. This arrangement already feels better. I should have handled it this way all along. "Would you like that?" I give her the opportunity to answer.

"Yes." She and I both say it at the same time. I want Shea to know that even that one small word isn't hers alone. Nothing is anymore. The phone in my pocket chimes and reminds us both why I am so angry.

"I don't want to be distracted. I'll come see you in the morning." And then, "Enjoy your dinner." I leave the light on in the room and shut the door without turning to check on her. I don't need to. The weeping starts as soon as the door shuts.

It helps to focus on tasks. I make myself a snack. I clear off a space on the table. Retrieve the box from the top shelf of the linen closet. Unpack my supplies and turn on the floor lamp so the light is brightest right above me. Then I get to work.

I keep the music off at first so that I can listen for movement in the back bedroom. First there's the crinkle of her unwrapping the sandwich. Then the creaking and occasional thuds of small movements, but nothing substantial. She doesn't have much space to move around.

It takes me three hours to complete and the rest of the night for the glue to dry, but I am thrilled with the final result. It's a showstopper of a gift—the kind of present that elicits gasps. It's worthy of an unboxing video. At the mall, I'd considered buying wrapping paper but decided that was too much. That's how carefully I consider every decision, how thoughtfully I care for Shea and me.

In the basket near the fireplace, Sonny keeps kindling and old newspapers. The sheets are yellowed with age, but they'll do just fine.

Maybe they even fit in with the whole retro vibe. I haven't wrapped a present for ages. Sonny just gives me gift cards for clothes and school supplies. Helen and I have a tradition where we do something together, rather than trade gifts. It's not the neatest job but at least it looks cheerful. It looks like a peace offering.

I stand at the bedroom door and hear Shea softly snoring. Outside, the sky is already lightening. I'm tired but I feel stronger than I have for some time. Resolved and determined. I even text Helen. I don't read her most recent messages but write *All okay here. Try not to worry. Just trying to make my own way.* And then because of course that will infuriate her, I add: *So much to explain when we have a chance to reconnect.*

My eyes twitch from squinting so much. At those tiny crystals. At the phone's screen. I lie back on the sofa and let my tired eyes rest.

CHAPTER 26

SHEA

When I wake up, I can tell by the warmth on my face that the sun's shining. My eyes twitch a bit from keeping them closed as long as possible. When I open them, the day will begin to unfold, probably in ways over which I have little control. I squint against the bright light. I try to prepare myself.

If my phone was in reach, I'd message my mom. I'd text Delancey. *Try not to worry,* I'd tell them. *I will find my way back. So much to explain when we reunite.*

Now I know for certain they're looking for me. That's the touchstone I return to. All yesterday, all last night. Someone understood my message. I'm gone only because I was taken. I've not returned only because I'm not free to go. I'm Alice in chains; I'm Alice gone down the rabbit hole. Go ask Alice— she'll tell you she wants to go home.

My head throbs in a foggy way. Nora's up to her old tricks,

but at least I can flex my arm and twist my wrist without wincing in pain. It looked like a break yesterday but maybe I overreacted. Today my arm aches but I can take it. I'm feeling stronger than I have in some time. Determined. Resolved.

The one thing I know for sure about today? It won't be yesterday. Yesterday played out like a nightmare—both a horror film and its sequel. My failed escape and then my arm versus a slamming door—the rematch. Nora's terrifying disintegration. And then the only thing worse. Her leaving.

Nora would point to it as proof of my narcissism, but sometimes it helps to imagine being interviewed about this ordeal. I compose careful answers. I try to take note of key details. Nora would say, *You do everything for an audience.*

But it helps to imagine eventually explaining it. I practice making sense of what's happening. In any case, if someone asked, I would tell them. I was never more afraid than after Nora left. At first you think it's a relief. The person who stays constantly at your side, who needs your approval for everything, finally steps away. Suddenly, you have space. You can breathe. Except you're handcuffed and she has the key. You can barely move. You're hungry and cold and then the darkness rolls in.

I thought Nora had opted for her exit strategy. Maybe she saw me hurt and panicked and decided to simply run. I'd scream and scream but eventually the vines and green would grow over the little cabin and seal me in; I would never be seen again.

The woman who interviews me might peer over her glasses

then. She'll ask, *Shea, did you think Nora left you alone to die at that moment?* And I will tell her. It was more than a moment. It was a moment that expanded into an hour and then stretched to a whole day.

It was a scream that I scraped into a bellow until my voice weakened to a rasp. I had quit and revived my efforts about twelve different times since the room had gone dark. By that time, I had decided to rest and then work to destroy the bed somehow. I thought I could drag it forward again and wear out the iron post against the wooden doorframe. Or try anyway.

Then I heard the truck rumble in, the footsteps scattering the gravel in the drive. The generator coughed and kicked in. Then eventually Nora stood in the doorway—flat and remote, but there.

It's hard to accept how relieved I felt to see her. How will I describe what happens here? Nora pelted me with a sandwich. I crawled under the bed to reach it. I knew it was dosed and still I devoured it. Lay back and let the thick waves of whatever pills she sprinkled on my food roll over me. It felt warm in the room for the first time in a while.

I touch my bad arm with my chin, checking for damage. I motivate myself with the memory of standing outside with the open sky stretching above me.

I brushed so close to finally getting away from here. And glimpsed exactly how it will go if I don't find a way out. When it's time and she's done with me, Nora will back her father's truck out of the drive. She'll leave me to scream until I am just an echo in the woods.

The doorknob turns and I fold into myself as much as possible. I peek out of my burrow to look for a phone in Nora's hand. *Please*, I want to beg, *do not take a video of me now*. I feel like a wild creature. My hair is not my hair anymore. Tears and strings of snot have dried in a crust on my face. There's a metal pail half-full of urine beside the bed. Nora could ruin me with one post. I know she has considered it. And maybe it is my own conceit, but it still matters to me. I'm desperately afraid two different ways—that Nora will film me and reveal me to the world. And that my fear means she's been right about me all along—I am an animal of vanity—self-obsessed and concerned only with appearances.

She steps into the room. "How are you feeling?" When I hear the question, I remember the new rule: I only get to answer Nora now. I count as less of a person. There's no more pretending we're friends on a weekend jaunt.

"I'm okay today, thank you." I am obedient. I watch and wait.

I must have spoken with a satisfactory amount of deference because Nora offers, "I promised you a shower." My eyes stay down, fixed on the floor. I try to look meek but not too eager. She clears her throat. Nora's not good at leading the conversation. She's trying like I'm trying. We both play parts. "Shea, would you like a shower?"

It's a risk because it's different. It could be a trick or a trap. I

227

try to run the math, but my brain still feels slack and slow. I go for the dream of hot water and clean hair: "Yes, please." I was never going to say no.

"Last night I worked out a system. A secure system. It's a great deal of effort. And the hot water demands a lot from the generator. It can't be a daily thing."

I've asked her for nothing. I almost nod before I remember that Nora has not actually asked a question. I wait, like a dog for a command. "Do you understand?" Nora's impatient with her own dumb game. But I stay docile. I comply.

"I do. Quick shower, however you instruct me." She nods and moves closer and steps back from the bedroom. I wait to see Nora's system, half expecting her to wheel in a giant cage or a metal gurney on which she'll strap me down.

She returns with a broom in her hand. That's Nora's sophisticated system of security. She wears a hoodie today and I can see the outline of a phone in her pocket. With one hand, she pulls the chain with the key over her neck. The other grips the broomstick: I see her knuckles whiten. I could reach out and grab the phone out of her pocket. It's close enough for me to reach even with my hands bound in front of me. But I don't have a plan for after. So I watch the weight of the phone swing forward. I think of the text I would send my mom: *So much to explain.*

Maybe Nora and I are both thinking of last time. She moves with purpose, but I know now how you work up the nerve to accomplish the frightening thing. It seems insane to imagine that's who I am to Nora. No matter how broken I am, she's still afraid I will overpower her.

Her hands tremble, the tiniest bit. I work to keep the smirk off my face. She moves fast; maybe she practiced again. Last night while I drifted in and out, Nora reviewed her kidnapping skills. She unlocks the handcuffs from the bed and switches the one loop to the broomstick. So now my hands are bound in front of me and then again to the wooden pole she holds in front of her.

The pole gives her more leverage. She can lean forward; that force pushes my whole body ahead. It's a small shower stall. Nora nods for me to step in the tub and so I do, fully clothed and fairly confused. I try to look casually around as if I am appreciating the decor and not searching for any item that might function as a weapon. Nora has renovated: no more metal towel rack, no soap dish. She's removed the mirrored door of the medicine cabinet. All around me are smooth tiles and floral wallpaper. Nothing to grip to keep from falling, let alone an errant razor left miraculously on the tub's edge.

Nora unhooks my hands in front of me and brandishes the broomstick like a weapon. "Now, quickly remove your shirt," she barks. I'm startled enough to twist out of my shirt and sports bra. Even though my arm vibrates with pain. Even though I'm unchained for a tiny sliver of time. I hesitate, trying to map out every possibility, and the slim window of opportunity slams shut. Nora connects my wrist to the safety rail on the side of the tub with a grim snap. Besides the faucets, that counts as the only metal in the tiny room. "That rail is designed to stay put." So am I, apparently.

She slides the broom out of the second set of handcuffs. "I'm going to step out now and wait outside. I'll stand on the other side of the door. You should take care when the tile gets wet. It will be more slippery. You don't want to fall. How's your balance?" I lift my untethered arm into fifth position and give her a small smile. I raise my chin the way Madame Flint taught.

"Okay, don't get overconfident. You're weak and confused," Nora informs me. "I'm setting the timer on my phone for five minutes. More than that and we'll need gas for the generator sooner than we can afford. And too much time might tempt you to make trouble." She looks at me sternly. "Shea, you're not going to make trouble?" It's both an instruction and a question. I risk a nod. Nora nods back like we just shook on an agreement, then closes another door between us.

Five minutes. I shimmy out of the rest of my clothes, leaning against the wall for support. I don't waste time looking at the rainbow of bruises purpling my arm. I've already had enough time to stare at myself. I turn on the tap and let the water run until it warms and then I switch on the shower. With the water rushing and drowning out sound, I allow myself three strong tugs on the metal safety rail. I pull at the drain. Nothing budges.

Nora raps on the door. "Two minutes." I feel the sobs climbing up my throat. I let the water fall on my face and wash away the hot tears. There's no shampoo but I soap and rinse myself, all the while apologizing. I hear the eventual interviewer in my head: "Wasn't there an opportunity to escape? And yet you chose a hot shower?"

I turn off the water before she has to tell me. Nora's left a towel folded on the toilet. I wrap it mostly around myself and wait for the door to open. Nora muscles forward, brandishing her broomstick. She moves to make the switch with the hand-cuffs. I imagine crouching down, throwing my shoulder into her and toppling us both. But I'm docile, clutching the towel around me and letting Nora work a flannel shirt over my head and arm.

She tells me, "There are more clean clothes for you in the living room. I think the rig will allow you enough movement to finish getting dressed." I follow her there and stand. I wait politely for Nora to fasten the chains. Maybe someday, someone will ask me, *Is it true you just stood there and allowed yourself to be chained?* It's hard to describe what happens here, to explain the rules by which Nora and I live.

All I can feel in this moment is grateful for clean clothes that smell good and hopeful that Nora will let her guard down. She will slip again in some small way and that will be a better moment to pounce. Or I'll hear another set of tires spray the small pebbles of the driveway and know that someone has finally succeeded in tracking us down.

Until then I relish the socks Nora has set out for me. They

are thick and white. I maneuver into the rest of the clothes. She sets a brush on the floor beside me.

"Would you like me to brush your hair?" she asks.

I would like Nora to not touch me. But I understand there's a danger in appearing unappreciative. "Yes, please. If you don't mind, thank you." It means I have to sit with my back to her then and feel Nora's hands in my hair. She works the damp strands into two braids close to my scalp. It's my favorite way to wear my hair. Another thing Nora knows about me. More of myself that I've given away online, without ever thinking that one day I might want every last sliver of my privacy back.

I have behaved well, sitting still and fully cooperating because Nora stands then and announces, "All set. It looks great. I think I got them close to the way you usually wear your braids." At home Delancey braids my hair. They hate when I flinch, so I hold perfectly still. It feels like I am betraying everyone at home when I feel the plaits in my own hair and say, "Wow. Nora, they feel so straight. Thank you."

Nora beams at me. And then she says, "Hold on a second. I have something for you."

She's wrapped the package and everything—in newspaper, but she's even fashioned a bow from scraps of paper twisted together.

"I don't understand," I say. I don't. "That's so kind of you." I question. "Especially after how I acted yesterday." I simper. "I really don't know what came over me. I just suddenly felt so homesick. I wasn't thinking at all." Nora stares at me, looking satisfied, and I keep chattering as I struggle to tear off the paper.

I've unwrapped a shoebox. I open it to see what is easily the coolest pair of sneakers I've ever actually held in my hand. They're vintage Nike Dunk Low Pure Platinums. Deadstock, from what I can tell, never worn. And they are covered in Swarovski crystals. I hold them up and tip them so that they catch the light. They glimmer and I legit gasp.

Nora laughs. "You like them."

"Like them? I love them." I look up at her. I don't know what to say. They are exactly my size—maybe more information that I posted hoping someone would send me freebies. I think back to that previous life, when I could not have imagined how complicated receiving a gift might be.

But now I know. "I can't keep them," I tell Nora. What I mean is *I won't hate you less*. "You should wear them." Because that is what I'd say to Delancey if they presented me with such an obscenely generous gift.

Nora shakes her head. She looks sad or wistful or some other emotion I haven't yet learned to decipher completely. "No way. Those are sneakers for a star. I'm not there yet." I open my mouth to argue, but Nora says, "No, that's okay, Shea. You worked for years for your recognition. It was unfair of me to expect to reach that level right away."

"You'll get there, Nora." And then I wince. I sound like a pretentious monster. And I spoke without waiting for a question.

But Nora doesn't seem to notice. "Yeah," she says, sounding unconvinced. "Right now, I'm just really tired—up late last night and all. I'm going to go in the back room and rest. But we should record a video later. Otherwise, the trolls will think they got to me. You did an early U2, remember—it really kicked off your whole turn to punk and glam. We could do a callback to that. Or something totally different. Maybe some Pixies? 'Gouge Away' has a line about chains. Do you know that one?"

"I don't think so. We don't have to do a line about chains," I say very carefully.

"Well, it's your channel too, right? We should both be able to communicate. Do you want to hear the Pixies song?"

"Sure. Okay, Nora." The air in the room has changed, almost imperceptibly. I'm walking a tightrope again, trying not to stumble into the hot vat of Nora's anger. We sit there, on the living room floor, my phone between us, its volume turned up. Nora presses all the buttons, brings up the song. "Where did you find this one?" I ask as if it's a casual, conversational question. As if I'm not trying to decipher the lyrics just like I hope our followers will at home. I risk talking out of turn.

"I spent a lot of time last night searching for the right song. The title grabbed me."

"Yeah?"

"Here, listen again." Nora hits play again, and I try to listen more closely. What am I missing? There's a line about breaking an arm, there's the description of chains. Nora insists, "I just really love the bass line."

"Right. Me too. It's a good choice, Nora."

"You think you can choreograph something?"

"You mean for both of us, right?"

"Yeah, for both of us. Just think about it a little bit and then we can work out the routine after I've had a chance to rest." She turns toward the bedroom and then turns back to me. "You should let the glue dry on the sneakers a little while longer. Okay?"

"Sure. Of course. You added the crystals?"

Nora nods slowly, and at first I think she's angry that I asked the question, spoke out of turn. But she says, "I wanted you to have something special. I designed them just for you."

"Thanks again." She turns away and I feel strangely desperate for Nora to stay. In an interview, I'd be asked to clarify: *You wanted your captor to stay and keep you company?* I would try to explain. *She's the only person I've talked to for days and I am so lonesome.* But Nora says she needs rest. I listen rather than risk another outburst.

Nora disappears into the back room. I hum the song and walk through plans. I measure steps and do my best to showcase Nora's movements. Anything to protect her from the contempt of our commenters who don't realize they endanger me when they upset the lumbering girl dancing alongside me.

When I get restless, I open the box and marvel again at the

Nikes. Nora's unhinged and all, but these sneakers would have been impossible to find. They must be a limited edition. If someone recognizes them on TikTok, maybe they can trace them to Nora. And then maybe they can trace Nora to me. I glance back at the shut door. It's been a shockingly hopeful morning. What could it harm to try the sneakers on?

I stand and lean on the sofa. I ease my foot into the leather shoe and feel a strange resistance. They're new, after all, and maybe they need breaking in. I push my toes forward and feel a searing pain on the sole of my foot. I yank my foot out to see red blood blooming against the white cotton of my sock. I shriek before I can stop myself, fling off the shoe and search for something to stanch the blood. That's when I look up and see Nora standing in the doorway, staring at me. I ask the question before I remember that I'm not allowed to ask questions.

"What did you do, Nora? What did you do?"

CHAPTER 27
NORA

When I hear Shea scream and see the smear of blood on the floor, I know immediately what she's done. She didn't listen. Even though I asked her to wait, Shea is so spoiled and impatient. Of course, she's gone and injured herself. "Have you hurt yourself, Shea?" I ask before I can stop myself. I hear the cold spite in my voice and watch her face crumple like a white cotton handkerchief. My own calm shocks me. "Put them both on," I order her, and reach for the metal poker next to the fireplace.

If I'm completely honest, I'm not sure when the glass shards went from a vague idea to an actual plan. Had Shea just let me sleep a little, I might have woken up refreshed and reasonable. I might have sat with the shoes and a set of tweezers and retrieved the slivers I built into the lining. But Shea never listens. She's never willing to follow someone else's timeline. I tried to give her everything this morning and she still couldn't follow a simple request.

Yesterday, I considered the broken glass as a last resort, protection in case someone managed to decipher more of Shea's coded videos. It helped my confidence to remember I can outsmart her. It can get frightening to be this isolated alone in the woods with someone as volatile as Shea. She is desperate and her behavior has escalated. To keep us both safe, I couldn't be taken by surprise again.

Then I sat at the table with superglue and the sneakers. It took focus to position each crystal just right. Each time I moved the tweezers and pressed down, I thought of a different vicious comment, another follower who wished I would simply disappear just so Shea could fit better into the frame. I thought of the ways she betrayed me. I felt those slights as cuts after all. Maybe now it's Shea's turn to bleed a little. "Put on your new sneakers. We need to record another video."

I keep my voice strong, the way I've practiced. I maintain eye contact and don't look down at the blossoms of blood stamping the wooden beams of the floor. It seemed like a harmless prank, but the sight of blood makes me woozy. Shea stares at me, imploring me. But I won't let her sway my plans. "'Gouge Away'—it's a great song, right? It's got a strong beat and completes the story you've told about you and me."

CHAPTER 28
DELANCEY

At the police station, Dad, Kallie, and I have told the same story again and again, to anyone willing to listen. I've frozen each frame to name every piece of evidence we've gathered from the latest video.

"It's a great song," this latest, younger cop says. "It's got a strong beat, but I'm not sure what you mean about a secret message."

It took long enough to convince Dad and Kallie, but even their arguments to the officers don't seem to gain traction. There's no action to take. We wait.

"My daughter is so smart. She takes her responsibilities seriously." Kallie keeps talking like she's helping Shea apply to college. She's not helping our cause at all.

Standing in the doorway, the police chief, who Kallie demanded to see, nods politely. "Now help me understand, folks," he says. "You suppose your daughter is being held captive by this other girl? You think she's chained up but we can't see those chains because the video has been edited? Do any of you recognize this young woman? The dancer in the back?"

I say, "Vaguely. I think she's a follower."

"This girl was following Shea?"

"Online. She was following online. But also, in person."

The police chief looks perplexed.

Even my dad rubs his eyes. "Delancey can take you through the video and show you the visual effects. Once you see it—it's clear as day." The police officers do not leap at the chance to look at our evidence of invisible chains. Dad tries a different approach. "Has anyone reported this other girl missing?" The chief exchanges glances with the younger officer. Dad seizes on the moment. "Well? Then I take it that her people are worried for her too?"

"We do have word of another missing girl. From the western part of the state. Matching description, but then Shea also matches that same description." The chief raises his hands as if to quell my dad's enthusiasm. "It's not an official report from a parent—just a phone call from a woman who hasn't had eyes on her younger sister for a few days."

"Did she give an address?"

The police chief glances down and shifts in his shiny black shoes.

Shea's mom leans forward and grips the sides of the conference table in front of us. I thought Dad and I should have just come to the station on our own. But Kallie lost it when I explained why the dance team and I thought Shea might be chained up somehow. Dad didn't think we could leave Kallie alone at the house. Now she's got them fixated on this other girl. What I need is someone who knows Photoshop well, who can help undo some of the video's doctoring.

Kallie asks, "Isn't a wellness check in order? My daughter is ambitious. She would not simply disappear in the middle of the school term."

"Ma'am, I can't run wellness checks for unauthorized slumber parties. Here is the thing: The address provided to us is very remote. However, given this new information, we will consider the possibility of sending an officer out to check in on the address provided."

"Give us the address. We'll do it tonight," Dad says. The atmosphere in the room changes. The younger officer, the one who likes grunge music, looks up at my dad with interest.

"Now you know I can't authorize that," the chief says. "We don't know that these two issues are related. I—"

"Put me on the phone with the lady in California. Doesn't matter if they're related. We know exactly how she's feeling. We're happy to drive out to—"

"I can't do that, sir."

"What has to happen?" Kallie asks in her wistful way.

"Ma'am?"

"How badly does my child need to be hurt for it to warrant a drive out of Pierce County?"

"No one indicated that, ma'am. But, in fact, we would need some kind of probable cause—"

"Does she need to have a visible injury?" The younger officer looks down at his keyboard; the police chief coughs into his hand. Kallie keeps speaking: "I just want to be clear how badly my daughter needs to appear hurt on video to warrant your interest."

"I'm really sorry, ma'am. I can imagine how frustrating and frightening this must be. I have to admit—I'm not seeing what y'all are seeing on this video. I see two girls dancing, having a good time goofing off, when maybe they should be thinking more carefully about the toll this has taken on their families." He raises his voice, to ward off our arguments. "We've sent out the video. If our tech department lands on the same conclusion that you have about editing out relevant details, we will immediately reach out to you. At that point, we would certainly work a different angle in the case."

Kallie sighs. She sinks back into her chair and opens her phone. "Maybe if you could just take a few moments to detect the way my vibrant daughter has faded over the past several days. She's clearly not well. Her skin tone is sallow; she's dropped weight."

"I'm sure you understand that I cannot sit here and watch your daughter's music videos. Again."

"Does she need to be bleeding?" Kallie asks.

My father reaches down to pat her arm. "All right, honey, you've made your point. We've tried our best here. They're going to pursue whatever leads they can. And you know we can look into hiring our own technicians. We'll have the video privately analyzed if we need to . . ." Dad trails off, in problem-solving mode. Kallie raises her hand up with the phone open and the sound on. I can faintly hear the tinny sound of music.

"Is that the Pixies?" The younger cop sounds impressed.

Kallie's voice drips with scorn. "How much blood before you make an effort to protect my daughter?"

We all swivel our heads to face Kallie then and the silver phone she holds up in the air. The younger officer seems to understand first and reaches for the cell phone. Kallie grips it tightly, but he says, more calmly and gently than any of the rest of us, "Ma'am, why don't you let me bring this up on my computer? This is her TikTok account, correct? We all can watch on the larger screen." A few taps on his keyboard and then Shea stands in front of us on the monitor.

This video looks very different from the earlier ones. It's more makeshift, less polished. The other girl poses in the background, but only Shea dances. She's wearing new clothes. The editing job on this one is more obvious. Someone hacked out a clear trail from the wall to Shea's left arm. Whoever edited it didn't take the time to hide any inconsistencies in the images. It's just a blurred line. I tap the screen and trace it. "I see what you mean. It could be a rope," the young officer says. "Or a chain." He taps a combination of buttons and screenshots the image. He looks up at the chief. "Are you tracking this, sir? There's something else worth considering; this song is called 'Gouge Away.'" The young officer hesitates, glancing at his audience. "With that context, I want to draw your attention to this, sir."

He highlights an area of the floor with his cursor. It's got the same distortion. And then it's like the video blinks. There's a glitch where the editing didn't quite take. Streaks of blood appear on the floor and then disappear in the next frame.

"Was that blood?" my dad asks quietly, his hand clasping Kallie's shoulder.

"It looks like something. Someone tried to edit that part out. A small pool on the floor, right corner." The officer takes more screenshots. The chief strides to a far desk and picks up a phone. More police stream into the small room. Around me, the station becomes busy.

I keep my focus on the screen. Both Shea and the other girl wear their hair in braids. Usually, I'm the one to braid Shea's hair. She sits in front of me with the TV on to distract from all the tugging. When she dances in this video, she keeps touching her hair. Her hands flutter to her braids. I want to believe that means she knows I'm picking up her signals. I hope she understands she's reaching me.

It's difficult to watch now that we're certain she's being held, now that we believe she's been hurt. We all see the dance differently now, understanding it as a sacrifice. Shea bares her teeth in an unwavering smile. She dances with determination. Her jaw is set, and she moves deliberately, almost robotically.

Each time she jumps with her left foot, she appears to hesitate. Then she forces her foot down, completing the step.

We lean closer to the screen to see. In the corner behind the other girl, I notice scraps of paper crumpled on the floor. "Is that a newspaper? Maybe it's local? Can you zoom in?" The assembled crowd bends forward and looks past the pain etched on Shea's face. Instead, we watch the officer try to magnify the scraps of yellowed pages on the floor, one more visible clue.

CHAPTER 29

NORA

Sitting at the kitchen table, I lean in closer to the phone's tiny screen. I rushed through the editing job, and it shows. This last video is difficult to watch; I see every defect now that "Gouge Away" has already posted. Usually, I prefer to take my time, to deliberate each shot.

Once when I only knew her from a distance, I tuned in for an "Ask Me Anything with Shea Davison." Another follower asked what she loved about choreography and I remember that Shea said she loved puzzling through it. She loved the challenge of finding the movement that perfectly fits a particular lyric, the exact sequence that matches a song just so.

I feel that way about cutting video. We make an amazing team, Shea and me. She can create the content and I can help her package it properly. This partnership will free her from worrying about those other details, the ones that weigh her down and kill her creative spirit. She can focus fully on what she loves. Maybe we've learned that I don't even need to dance—I'm possibly more of a director than a performer. With any luck, that's something Shea and I will still have the chance to work through together.

Right now, I'm working through significant frustration. Shea keeps weeping behind me, and that's honestly very distracting. So much so that I posted this last video without one final review. That's an accidental post with substantial consequences. My edits of the rig are problematic, for one. If you're looking for it, and some of our followers are certainly searching, you can see the ghost of the rig swinging from the ceiling. It surfaces as a blurry stretch of background attached to Shea, limiting her movement.

In the "Would?" video, I took my time with the eraser brush; without Shea's mischief, everyone would have overlooked it. But I hurried through the process for the Pixies song—I was careless and left an outline. Anyone could notice.

Then there is the blood. I missed one frame, maybe three. But the gore is jarring. You blink and a quick footprint of blood stains the wood floor.

It hurts me to see it. I meant to scare Shea, that's all. To remind her that I am a person to be appreciated. I'd played it out so differently in my head. I thought she would slip her feet into the sneakers and maybe nick her heel or scrape her toe. I thought it might slow her down, lower those leaps. I didn't expect that Shea would push against that pain and keep going. I didn't anticipate that she would dance through until she'd cut herself all up.

Now words like *assault* and *kidnapping* keep popping up on the screen. I force myself to count to three and breathe in. Count to three and exhale. Shea's injured—I see that, but we can handle it with the first aid kit and some time off her feet.

It was a foolish thing to do—it was a dumb prank. I can't see how it counts as *assault*.

Shea's stubbornness has undone us. She is so proud of her discipline and strength. But all of us are meant to eventually relent. Now blood seeps from the glittering white soles of her new shoes. She's ruined them. All that time I spent making them perfect, and she's ruined them. I need to figure out what to do next. Shea mews and whimpers and sops up the blood with the rag I threw down. But now I can't do much more than that. After all, the comments are coming through. They need my attention too.

The words scroll fast and insistent, asking about the extent of Shea's injuries. Her followers call me cruel names; they make outlandish claims. They point to how Shea's face has drained of color and of course ask about the blood seeping into the floorboards. I try to type quickly: *Appreciate your care. We're exploring special effects over here.*

No way. Reporting this video for content. Team Shea: Call 9-1-1, okay?

Already called. Hey, Othergirl, cops on their way.

We love you, Shea. Reported for content. Hoping you'll get home safe.

Call 9-1-1. Time to Gouge out Othergirl.

I try not to panic—it's just a few troublemakers, melodramatic content creators themselves. I try for a cheerful, helpful tone. *BTW, Shea thinks this misunderstanding is hilarious.*

Devo responds directly to my post. *Then put Shea on live. Give her the mic.*

My eyes run over the typed line of Devo's comment, trace the shape of the letters. Devo needles me. But it might be the one way to slow down the situation, to buy me and Shea some time for healing. We'll take a break from posting. And then we'll launch a comeback.

"They want to see you, Shea. Our followers love you. All these comments—they're checking to make sure you're okay."

Shea looks up at me slowly, as if she can't quite decipher my language.

"I am not okay, Nora." Shea's voice shakes.

"You went too far," I chastise. Then I confess, "And I went there too. I'm so sorry about the shoes, but I never expected you to keep dancing. You're so successful but you feed this need to constantly prove yourself. We both have this artistic mentality. We use ourselves up." I start straightening the backdrop. I grab the rag and start swiping away some of the blood from the floor.

"Let's make it quick," I tell her. "Nothing elaborate. Just a check-in to cheer up folks who may have been disturbed. We pushed boundaries. Artists do that, right? We just need to acknowledge that last video went too far." I crouch down to her and hold the camera up, cropping out Shea's entire left side. That's the best angle. That's the right shot.

"You want to make a video? Now?" I hear the disbelief in Shea's voice. But I don't have time for convincing. I have one eye on the comments section. Devo has veered out of control, calling for TikTok to stop broadcasting our content. Challenging hackers to trace our location.

And then there are the texts from Helen. Ten, eleven of them. Somehow, she's found out Shea's name.

Just stay right there at the cabin, Nora. What have you done? On my way.

I keep my voice even. I need to stay steady for Shea. "I don't want to alarm you," I say calmly. "It's been an emotional morning. But there's commenters calling for you to get canceled. They want a trigger warning for violence. Let's give them twenty seconds, tops. Just something to reassure our followers. We'll show that you're just fine and that our partnership is strong."

Shea considers it. "They'll just tear this one apart too." She shakes her head, sounding dejected. "I don't know if I can stand to see it anymore. We need an unexpected feature—something to drive views hard."

"We could go live?" I say it and know that's exactly what

we need to do. It will prove that Shea's just fine, that what we're doing here for the channel is meant to benefit both of us. It will reestablish the two of us as collaborators, co-creators.

I haven't trusted Shea enough. I see that now. That has almost undone our partnership—all my efforts. I work as fast as I can. I unlatch Shea from the rig and attach us together at our wrist. This closes the distance between us, connects us once again. In the front pocket of my hoodie, both phones vibrate against each other. It feels like a flood of notifications, a tidal wave of public commentary crashing over us.

I have to look. I need to see what they're all saying. I tap the screen. At first glance, I don't believe it, so I spread my fingers across the tiny display. As if increasing the font size might magically transform the messaging: *Packwood, Washington.* Somehow, they've found the closest town to us. Below that Devo writes *Hold on, Shea. Stay strong* and then *Othergirl, we're coming for you.*

CHAPTER 30

SHEA

I haven't trusted myself enough. I see that now. Nora has overpowered me because I've allowed her to do so. It's almost undone me—but I remember now. She's got me bound to her by the wrist again. I hate the loss of space, being this close to her, the wisps of her hair that brush against my face. I feel sick breathing in Nora's exhaled air.

But it lets me notice more. She's distracted, unraveling. Standing next to Nora, I hear that her breath is ragged. I need to stay steady. I ready myself. All this time I've misunderstood the phones as tools to use against her. I've thought of placing a call or sending a text, requesting help. But I understand now how I can use the phones to my advantage. Every time they chime or buzz, the two phones in Nora's pocket offer a diversion. She cannot turn away from them.

This last time Nora checked her phone, it opened a new set

of options—the wide sky, the cold woods, white pines on either side, as far as I can see. Nora won't say what she read in the comments of our latest malevolent masterpiece. But it spooked her enough to bundle me up and out the cabin's front door. To bypass the truck in the drive and trek outside without any clear direction.

"Nora, where are we going?" When she shakes her head, her temple grazes mine. She jerks in reaction and loosens her grip on my arm. I can afford to step back only a little. I take care to not pull away. Nora needs to believe I would stay.

I know her so well now. I've studied her the way she's studied me. She says, "Just a walk. We've been so cooped up." But Nora looks back and checks the phone every few seconds. I stop myself from following her gaze. The phone doesn't matter to me anymore. It's just a trapdoor that Nora might fall into. I work hard to keep up with her pace so that she doesn't have to pull me along.

I have underestimated my own strength. It's freezing outside. The ground crunches with frost under our feet and the leaves are slippery. With each movement, I feel hobbled by pain. My legs feel weak, my feet bleed. But I don't need to show Nora all that extreme suffering.

I decide that these woods are just another stage. After all, I've trained for years to perform. My poor feet are already so calloused from toe shoes. Training for years. I hardly feel the gashes that bleed. For just a little while, I let myself forget, but my own

legs remember working through agony. I lean on that now—
that muscle memory.

Nora talks a big game about survival skills, but I know how
soft she is. She lacks focus and discipline. Every time a phone
chimes, I feel her tremble through the metal between us. There's
something she's not telling me.

During recitals, it's vital to ride the wave of adrenaline when
it hits you. Otherwise, when the fear kicks in, your body reacts
in ways that don't serve your training. Your knees knock, your
arms shiver. All that quivering interferes with the precise movements that the dance demands.

It's freezing and I'm bleeding and probably going into shock
in the near future. I won't waste my adrenaline waiting for
someone else to rescue me. When we reach a small clearing, I
let myself tear up and whimper about my feet. "Nora, can you
give me a sec?" I whimper pitifully. "My feet—I just want to
check . . ." She bends to let me kneel down. And then.

I reach down and wrench the piece of glass from the side of
my right sneaker. I moved it there as soon as I could and let Nora
think it was still in my foot. It's smooth and wet and hard to grip. I
lunge at Nora with the force of a grand jeté. I clutch the glass shard
and slash at her wrist. I had thought I might hesitate, but it turns
out I miscalculated my own rage. I hear her yell my name and I
tackle her down. We tangle on the ground and it's easier than I
expected to pin Nora beneath my knees. I'm not even panting.

She bucks and strains but really, she's barely fighting me off.

Nora looks up at me and then she does her worst. She dares to look hurt.

"I'm so tired of you," she spits out. "I've given up years just listening to you talk about your life. No one has ever given up so much just to spend time with you, Shea."

You don't need to listen when someone else tells you who you are.

With one hand, I press the glass against Nora's wrist. With the other, I snap the necklace off her neck. I move the sharpest edge to rest against the vein flickering at her throat. "You need to use this key to unlock the handcuffs," I instruct her carefully. At some point, the snow started falling. While Nora unlocks me, I watch tiny flakes swirl around us both. My wrist feels weightless. We are both smeared with blood.

And then I am falling backward. I let myself drift for a split second and Nora shoves me off her. I roll to my feet to see her scrabble on her back along the ground. She's reaching through the snow and dead leaves for something. Now that scares me. I track her movements and follow her hands, searching for a weapon or some element I missed. But then Nora staggers to her feet, clutching my phone in her hand.

Above us, the wind picks up in a swirling squall. My ears ache from the cold air. Snowflakes settle in Nora's hair, even on her eyelashes. But it's not a storm that gusts above us. We look up to see a helicopter circling. I need to fight for just a little while longer; help is already hovering.

It's almost like we call a truce for a second. We stand and watch the aircraft duck and dip above the pine and spruce. Nora stares at the sky and then at me. She cries. I wonder if Helen has arrived back at the cabin. Or if it's my mom and Delancey parked behind Sonny's truck in the drive. If I could think of anything, I'd say something kind.

Nora holds up my phone and yells, "You wanted a live video, Shea! Hey there, followers, it's me—Othergirl. Listen, it's just about the end of this collaboration odyssey for Shea Davison and me. You've been refreshingly honest with your feedback, so I feel it's only fair to drop a few truth bombs myself. Because I'm one of you. You love Shea. Me too. I've watched her every day for years."

My rescuers may be near, but Nora won't let go of this last chance to rack up views. She turns her back to me so that we're both in the frame. All the ways I was brave today, but this freezes me. I stare up into the camera and wonder how many people are tuning in to see Nora demolishing me.

I drop the piece of glass. I don't want people to see me that way.

"I thought we had so much in common—Shea Davison and me. But Shea's mostly interested in what she can get for free, who she can use up on her climb to the top. I thought she was so courageous, caring for her depressed mom, dancing through her *difficult feelings*. Shea just wants attention. That's why she's so bitter now that her mom's remarrying. She won't get to use her mom's depression as her own trademarked tragedy. What will Shea survive next? A very rich stepdad? Tune in tomorrow, followers!"

"No!" I find myself calling out, even though I know deep down there's no point in arguing. "That's not true."

"Just look back yourselves. Review the tapes. Read the receipts. Watch all her posts again. Because I have, and now I get it. Shea Davison is self-centered and spoiled. She doesn't care about you," Nora rants. "Shea doesn't even bother to read your comments. You all called me a kidnapper, but I had to hold her captive just so that she would notice me. We mean nothing to her. Shea is an empty shell of a human—a human turned internet commodity."

Maybe Nora is right and that's exactly what I am. Because that empty shell of myself fills up with so much anger and outrage. I cannot listen anymore. I can't allow to her to keep speaking for everyone in the world to see. I rush toward Nora, straight at the camera, and knock her down into the snow. She fights me. We yank braids and brawl and spit out each other's names. No chains. No glass. It's just Nora and me and all the and anger between us. We wrestle for control and I finally wrap my fingers around the prize. Then I pound her hand on the roots of a tree.

Finally, I'm able to pry Nora's hands from my phone.

I hold the familiar weight of it in my hand without pressing any buttons. I don't speak into the screen. I don't call for help or text in code. I hold it up so Nora has one final look at the tiny amount of power she took from me. I smash the phone again and again on a flat white rock between us. I watch the case shatter and the parts inside fragment. "No!" Nora wails with grief, as if I've torn her dream to pieces. And I suppose I have, there in the cold woods.

It stuns me, how much pain the phone's destruction brings. Nora screams and wails. I hear her cries and can't help feeling sorry for all the hurt rising through her. She must have felt so alone. Then she found me on a tiny screen. Who am I to say that shouldn't mean something? Nora throws back her head and howls. Then her mouth stays open, and another sound drowns out everything.

The helicopter thunders and whirs on its approach. It kicks up a swirl of wind and debris. I don't even see it land because I shield my face with my hands.

I don't see her stand and flee. In the chaos of rescue, I lose sight of her. The tall pines take her in. I fight to sit up. I crane my neck to see but the helicopter men gently push me down, tell me to stay down.

"You're safe now," they tell me. They use my name, claim that my mom is on her way. My head spins to see where Nora could be. The woods have swallowed her up. Snow settles over her footprints. The rescue team bandages my wrists. They peel off my bloody shoes and socks and fit my arm into a splint. They work over my body as if it is a thing that is not my own.

All I can think to say is, "I want to go home."

By the time we start making our way back to the cabin, Nora is long gone. "You have to search for her." I beg and plead. They ask me for her name, her age, identifying details. One of the rescuers speaks into her walkie-talkie. "Stand by for a description of the other girl."

When I describe her, Nora sounds just like me.

CHAPTER 31

NORA'S PHONE

Days later, the search party has found few traces of Nora Monahan in the deep woods of Eastern Washington. On the fourth day, an officer reports a possible lead. He stakes a yellow flag by the banks of a stream winding into the wintry wilderness where he located what looks to be Nora's phone. It's low on battery but still works.

One quick look at the screen reveals a photo of two girls in their teens. Both Nora and Shea smile widely up at the camera. Shea's arm is wrapped around Nora's shoulders and Nora holds an autographed Washington State Fair program. In the background the lights of the Ferris wheel glow.

When interviewed, Ms. Davison does not recall taking the photo, but acknowledges she signed over a hundred autographs that night.

The last text message received is communication from Helen

Humbolt, believed to be the missing girl's sister. *Nora, I love you. Whatever's happened, we'll work through it together. On my way.* This message was left unread.

Other notifications highlight the live video that Nora posted from Shea's channel days before—the video now considered evidence.

With more than four million likes in less than a week, it's Shea Davison's most popular post by far.

ACKNOWLEDGMENTS

Thank you to Cormac and Maeve. For more than ten years now, you have been my every incentive. Since I was your age, I've dreamed of being a writer. It's a cool gig indeed, but nothing compares to being your mom.

Thank you to Rob Franzmann. His strength, love, and commitment are everything we needed.

And thank you to Banjo, who was committed to sitting beside me as I wrote these pages.

Love and gratitude to the Corrigan, McKay, Ryden, and Franzmann families. Thank you to my parents, John and Ber-, and my brother, John. And to Steve Loy—for more than thirty years, he has encouraged me through every phase of my life, even the awkward ones. This book is the first one I've written without talking through characters and plot twists with Anne Glennon. I miss her every day.

My little family is rooted in two communities: Tacoma, Washington, and Somerset, New Jersey. I am grateful for my friends near and far. Especially if we've weathered time and distance, please know that I follow and celebrate your triumphs: Rose Abondio, Sara Belyea, Joe Chodl, Sandra Forero Bush, Hannah Garrow, Annie Green, Lynn Hernandez, Lucy and Ruth Iwamoto, Ann Kansfield, Elijah Kaufman, Nicole Martone, Stacy McMillen, Billy Merrell, April Morecraft, Mark Nastus, Sara Nardulli, Ella Nowak, Sherry Riggi, Denise Ryan, Meredith Santowasso, Brian Selander, Nina Stotler, Jeremy Stubbs, Cora Turlish, and Emily and Bryan Weston. Thank you for all the ways you continue to influence me.

I am so incredibly fortunate that my books get to wear Christopher Stengel's amazing cover designs when they step out into the world. Thank you for the way your amazing talent enhances my writing. Thank you to the entire Scholastic team for providing me with the extraordinary chance to share my work with the world and for showcasing it with such skill.

And, of course, thank you to David Levithan—for providing me with a path to publishing when I was twenty-two, for believing in the immense power of poetry but also showing me the unexpected opportunities of novels. Thank you for standing by me through my questionable mid-twenties and later throwing me the lifeline of writing projects when I was a single mom with two babies and too many bills. Over and over, it's felt like you've saved me. Thank you for giving me the chance to rescue myself.

In the early morning hours, I work on my writing. Then I leave to spend my days with the remarkable students in the Upper School for Girls at Annie Wright Schools. My students are fiercely courageous, steadfastly compassionate, and intelligently adventurous. While none of my characters or storylines are based on our students and their lives, the USG inspires me every day. Thank you especially to Shea Davison and Kamalani Enomoto, who lent their names to this novel, and Nya Zae 1, who provided a dancer's perspective.

ABOUT THE AUTHOR

Eireann Corrigan's novels for YA readers include *Remedy, Creep, Accomplice, The Believing Game, Ordinary Ghosts,* and *Splintering.* She is also the author of the acclaimed YA memoir *You Remind Me of You.*